MASTERED BY THE BERSERKERS

LEE SAVINO

FREE BOOK

Get a secret Berserker book, Bred by the Berserkers (only to the awesomesauce fans on Lee's email list)
Click here to get started…https://geni.us/BredBerserker

MASTERED BY THE BERSERKERS

When I became a nun, I vowed to remain chaste and pure. Then the Berserkers raided the abbey and carried me off. Now I'm their captive, at their mercy. And no amount of prayer will stop the two giant, dominant warriors from claiming me as mate...

They will strip me of my vows and put me on my knees. They will make me burn with unholy desire. They will not stop until they've mastered my pleasure.

And, Heaven help me, when it's over, I'll beg for more.

Bless me, Father, for I have sinned. Over and over and over again.

PROLOGUE

The moon hung high in the sky, bathing everything in silvery light. I crouched against the outer wall of the lodge, pressing myself into the roughly hewn logs and shivering. It was early spring and there was still snow on the ground, but I wasn't cold.

Just the opposite. A bead of sweat rolled down my forehead, tickling my skin and soaking a stray tendril of my hair. With a trembling hand, I wiped it away.

The fever inside me burned on. A cruel fire, roasting me from the inside.

How many hours had I been outside this night? How many times this winter had the fever driven me outside? The first few times, I planted my face in the snow to cool it. Now I didn't bother.

Pleasepleaseplease, I prayed, as I had many nights before. *Kyrie eleison. Lord have mercy.*

But no help came. The moon glared at me in silent witness of my sins.

A crunch of gravel under a boot was my only warning

before a shadow fell across me. The one who cast it was tall and broad and larger than an ordinary man—a giant hewn from rock. A Berserker.

"Juliet." The giant shadow spoke. Behind him, to the right, another shadow glided over the frozen ground. A second warrior. Only a Berserker could be so large, yet move so silently.

"Jarl." I let my head fall back against the wall, stifling a groan. Of course my prayers wouldn't be answered this night. "And Fenrir."

As I named them, the warriors stepped into the light. Both were bearded and broad of shoulder, but Jarl was a bit broader, and Fenrir taller with longer hair.

"Juliet." Jarl cocked his head. "You're not wearing your boots."

I tucked my bare feet under my shift. "What do you want?" I croaked. No sense hiding the fact that they were bothering me.

"You know what we want." Jarl crouched down beside me. A strong scent, woodsmoke and pine, wound around me. I fought to keep myself from leaning into him. "You still suffer," he observed.

I laughed, my breath puffing in the cold air. "Some say suffering is a woman's lot."

"How long?" Jarl asked.

I licked my cracked lips. "You know how long. You've watched me all these months."

Jarl swore.

Fenrir frowned and came closer, but he remained standing. He crossed his arms over his chest and looked out over the silent forest, alert.

The clenched fist of my heart relaxed. Something about these men standing close, guarding me made me feel safer than I ever had. I didn't like it, but my body gave me no choice.

"You've suffered all these months. There is no need." Jarl reached out to brush my brow. "We've waited for you to come to us."

I had to fight my own instincts and force myself to duck away from his touch. "It's no use. I took a vow."

Jarl clenched his outstretched hand into a fist. "Does this vow require your death? Because we see it and know as well as you—the fever weakens you. You cannot survive it. You must submit to your lust."

I bared my teeth at him. "Never."

"Little one, you are not a nun anymore."

"I will always be a nun."

"Is your god so cruel he desires you to act against your own impulses?"

I closed my eyes to shut him out and whispered, "*The wages of sin is death. Blessed are they who are pure in heart, for they shall see God.*"

"It's no use," Fenrir said in a voice so deep, it was almost a growl. My eyes flew open.

Jarl rose. For a moment I was disappointed. I squashed that down. I was glad they were leaving. Truly.

But Jarl didn't leave. Neither did Fenrir. They glanced at each other and golden flames lit their eyes.

"Then you leave us no choice," Jarl said.

I scrambled upward. "What do you mean?"

His arm snapped out, and shackled my wrist before I could react. "You're coming with us."

I tugged, but couldn't break free from his awesome strength. It didn't help that his thumb feathered against my pulse and every touch weakened my limbs. "What?"

"This ends now," Fenrir said. He crowded me until I was caged between him and his warrior brother.

Jarl drew me close until my small frame brushed his. "We're taking you this night."

1

Juliet

I REMEMBER the night the Berserkers sacked the abbey.

I was slumbering on my pallet, my cold feet peeking out from my thin blanket, when a scream shook me from a dreamless sleep. I was up and on my feet before I knew I was awake. The screams came from all around, echoing from the very walls. Behind me, the nuns stirred on their beds.

I ran to the narrow window and that's when I saw them: giant, silent shapes thronging the abbey. Warriors. Bearded and hulking, moonlight glinting on their axes, knives, and swords. They were huge and half naked. A few carried torches. The rest were breaking down the doors, hunting their prey down the stone halls, dragging the young women from the orphanage onto the lawn.

The screams came from a young woman in her white shift, tossed over a warrior's shoulder. He strode from the abbey and disappeared into the forest.

My shriek died in my throat. This wasn't happening.

I raced to the door.

"Sister Juliet, stop," the abbess cried when I would unbar it.

"We must help them!" I shouted, and fought when one of the sisters clawed me, trying to drag me back. The rest of the sisters cowered in a corner.

"Fool girl," the abbess snarled. She wore only a night shift and her long grey hair was a pitifully thin rope down her back. "This is an invasion. We must save ourselves."

"My sisters are in trouble." I struggled with the attacking nun. Sister Hilda was large and round, with thick muscles from tilling the fields. She wrestled me to my knees. I gasped as my knees hit the flagstones. It seemed mad that we were fighting while the abbey was under attack.

"They are only orphans," the abbess said, looking down her nose at me. "We are your sisters now."

All fighting ceased when the barred door shuddered. Sister Hilda released me and we both scurried backwards, away from the splintering wood. The thick door offered not a minute of resistance. A few more seconds and the axes broke through.

Then large hands tore the door apart. The nuns behind me screamed as the hulking shapes filled the frame. Sister Hilda and the abbess fell back, but my feet would not move.

I stood between the warriors and their axes and the rest of my sister nuns. The men were even bigger than they looked from the window. They towered over me.

"Stop," I shouted. I don't know what possessed me, but I was seized with madness. "What is the meaning of this?"

They didn't answer. One sniffed the air, his head raised like a wolf. "Spaewife." Beside him stood a huge wolf—taller than me, its head bigger than mine. Another round of frightened cries went up from the nuns as the great creature slunk inside.

I spread my arms. I was shaking, but I held my ground. "You can't come in here. We are nuns. We are peaceful. We have given ourselves to God."

The warrior and wolf were almost upon me when two warriors pushed to the fore. One was tall and lean with long dark hair spilling down his back. He wore a fur pelt slung over his shoulder, leather breeches and nothing else. The second warrior was stockier but still huge. His arms were covered with dark designs and swirls.

"We come for the spaewives," he announced to the room at large. "We are taking them."

"Why?" I cried and he settled his disturbing gaze on me.

"No fear. We mean no harm."

"No harm?" I asked.

The tattooed warrior dipped his head. "You can go with the spaewives, if you wish."

"Begone from this place," the abbess cried. "Take those wicked girls and leave us in peace."

The tattooed warrior raised a brow. He exchanged a look with another warrior. The wolf at his side backed out of the room.

"Wait," I said. I couldn't believe what I was saying. Outside, a girl screamed, "Help!" briefly before the sound cut off.

I flinched and said quickly, "I will go."

"As you wish." The warrior drew close, and raised his head to sniff the wind. "You are a spaewife."

"I am Sister Juliet."

He said something to me, and I shook my head. I couldn't hear him over the din and distant screams.

"Little wife," he repeated and opened his hand to me.

I hesitated. Was I really going to do this?

Before I could back away the tattooed warrior grabbed my arm and wrenched me through the door. The second, long haired warrior followed.

Then the world tilted, and I screamed. The warrior had caught me up over his shoulder and carried me off.

"Put me down." I beat my fists upon his back. He only quickened his pace. We were in the forest, the abbey disappearing, crowded out by the thick canopy of tree branches.

I bit back a scream and tried to think. Fighting would do no good. Neither would shouting for help. Who would hear?

I would have to think. But I could not. My thoughts tumbled about. Perhaps I would open my eyes and find this all a dream.

A burst of cries in the distance had me craning my head to see where the warrior was taking me. There were torches ahead, in a clearing between the trees. There, a circle of warriors surrounded a group of young women in white shifts. I recognized them from the abbey orphanage.

The warrior who held me swung me down. I tried to stagger away from him, but he held my arm. Steadying me as well as keeping me close.

The group of girls saw me and turned, sobbing. I jerked toward them, fighting the warrior's grip. He gripped me harder, but when I reached for the girls, he let me go.

The orphan girls surrounded me, shaking and crying. A few warriors ranged around us in a loose circle. Others darted to and fro, entering the abbey and carrying out more orphans, adding to our number.

"There, there," I murmured. My throat was dry, but I

grabbed a young one and cuddled her close. "It will be all right."

"What is happening?" one girl named Meadow cried. A monstrous wolf brushed by her and she screamed, lurching away from it. Her cry was echoed amid the rest of the girls.

"I don't know." I swallowed my fear. "Hush now, be calm. Here, now, see to the young ones."

Tears tracked down Meadow's face, but she turned and obeyed, gathering two younger girls to her.

I shifted the girl I held to my other hip. She buried her face in my neck. "Shhh," I told her. Clover, that was her name. Another orphan, named by the nuns. She'd come to us as a babe, and I was the only mother she'd known.

The warrior who'd grabbed me hovered at my back. I turned to glare at him.

"What will you do to us?"

He stared at me a moment before speaking. The whorls and swirls of his tattoos went up his neck, and I found myself wondering why a man would mark his skin so. "It's all right," he said finally. "You have nothing to fear."

"No, of course not," I practically spit at the warrior. "You attack us in the middle of the night and drag us out of our beds. Why would we be afraid?"

He blinked. Then, slowly, a grin spread across his face. The grin made my pulse quicken, and I backed away, more disconcerted by his amusement and my reaction to it than the whole wild night.

"You are not afraid of me."

I swallowed my retort. I was afraid, wasn't I?

The warrior tilted his head to the side, studying me. "You have no boots."

I looked down at my bare feet. "Of course I have no boots," I said, exasperated.

The warrior opened his mouth to say more but the long-haired warrior nudged him. "We go."

"Go?" I asked, my voice sharp. "Go where?"

But the tattooed warrior only clamped his large hand on my upper arm and pulled me away.

∼

AND THEN FOLLOWED days of hell, as the warriors made us march to their mountain. The Berserker warriors were not unkind, but the days-long journey wore me to the bone. Often as not, I walked in the center of a ragged group of the orphan girls. Meadow helped me calm them and wipe away tears. At times the young ones grew so tired of walking, the warriors carried them.

"Who are they?" Meadow whispered to me one night when we lay down by the fire for a few hours rest. My calves ached and I couldn't feel my feet. I'd left the abbey in a shift and nothing else. I'd marched mile after mile barefoot.

"They are warriors. Northmen." I'd guessed as much from the tales I'd heard of tall, pale men who fought with axes and sailed dragon-headed ships. They were fearless and left slaughter in their wake. I could easily see these warriors as that dreaded horde. "They served as mercenaries and settled in the mountains."

"Did they tell you that?" Meadow's voice held awe.

"No." I could've asked. Two of the warriors were often at my side. From their conversations with other warriors, I learned the tattooed one's name—Jarl. The tall one who stalked me like a shadow was Fenrir. Whenever they were near, my skin prickled with awareness. But I ignored them as best I could.

Meadow chewed her lip, her eyes on the warriors sitting

around the fire. Every once in a while, a warrior would leave and a few minutes later, a wolf would stroll from the forest. I shivered at what that might mean.

"But why do they want us?" Meadow asked finally.

"I don't know." But deep down, I did. But it wasn't something a nun, especially one young as me, should think about.

I rolled away from Meadow and fell asleep, and when dawn came, I woke to a new pair of boots and a thick cloak sitting by my head. Both nicer items of clothing than I'd ever owned.

I put them on and they fit perfectly. When I looked up, Jarl was watching me from across the fire.

But I turned away. And neither he nor Fenrir said anything to me, though I knew they were responsible for the gifts. For the rest of the trip I refused to speak or even look at them. I would not thank them, or think of them, or acknowledge what their gifts might mean.

2

Juliet

"I HEARD THE WARRIORS TALKING. Laurel is with child." Meadow slouched next to my bed, chewing on her lip.

"Good for her." I swung down, wincing at the cold. Autumn came early in the mountains. I grabbed my cloak—the one Jarl and Fenrir had given me—and swung it around my shoulders. It was dark blue and lined with rabbit fur. Heavy and warm enough for me to wear through the winter.

It had been several moons since the Berserkers took us from our home. The orphans and I lived in a lodge nestled high in the peaks. We were surrounded by forest and meadow.

"I wish to visit her. Perhaps I could stay with her while she carries the babe," Meadow said, twisting a lock of her hair.

"Perhaps. I can ask our guards." There were always several stationed nearby our lodge. To keep others out, as much as to keep us in.

"They don't want us roaming far anymore," Rosalind said from her perch by the hearth. On the floor, her sister Aspen played with the girls her age—Violet, Briar, Juniper, and Clover. "They say it's too dangerous." She sniffed. "If these warriors are so strong, why don't they kill the Corpse King once and for all."

In the opposite corner, Fern gasped. I looked to her questioningly, but she'd shrunk into a ball, her red hair curtaining her face.

"We shouldn't speak of him," Meadow cautioned in a whisper.

"Who? The Corpse King?" Rosalind tossed her long blonde hair. "I'm not afraid."

Meadow stiffened.

"It's not a sin to be afraid," I said gently. I put my hand on Meadow's shoulder and she softened.

"Is that why you cower outside during the full moon?" Rosalind muttered under her breath.

It was my turn to stiffen. I opened my mouth to deny it, but my lips were frozen.

"Rosalind," Fern murmured, and the blonde girl shut her eyes. "I'm sorry. Juliet, I didn't mean it."

But what was done was done. What was said was said. My secret was out. Maybe it had never been a secret.

I rose, smoothing my dress down as regally as I could. Both Rosalind and Fern watched me, one wary, one saddened. Both had pity for me.

"I am going to fetch water," I told her. "Please watch the young ones. If they wish to go outside, do not let them stray."

"Do you need help?" Meadow bounced to her feet and smoothed back her hair. She always wanted to leave the safety of the lodge. Not to do chores or keep me company, but to catch the eye of a warrior. I often caught her preening near the outpost of our guard. She was still too timid to flirt outright, but it was only a matter of time.

I bit back my retort. "No, I wish to be alone."

Her face fell and I gentled my tone with a smile. "When I return, we will all go pick wildflowers. See that the little ones are dressed and put on their shoes."

I swept past Rosalind.

"I'm sorry," she said again as I passed her. I gripped her shoulder a moment, meaning to comfort, but unlike Meadow she didn't soften. That was just Rosalind. There was always something brittle in her. Like her beautiful face was made of clay—lovely, but one wrong move and she would shatter.

I didn't begrudge her moods. I felt the same as she did—worry, fear, distrust of our captors. Relief that we were warm and well fed. And, deeper still, an unease, an expectancy telling me it was only a matter of time before the Berserkers came for me again.

When I left the lodge, the tension broke from my shoulders like I'd doffed a heavy cloak. I'd been up a few times that night with Ivy and Clover, who were restless in sleep. Fern, too, often had nightmares. We were all still settling into our new home.

I took up the buckets and headed for the path leading to the stream. The clearing around the lodge was empty, and the forest was still, but I knew better. The back of my neck prickled with the awareness I had when a certain two warriors were near.

I hadn't gone five steps before a big shape moved out

from a tree. I caught my breath but didn't let my feet falter as the warrior named Jarl strolled to my side.

"Little wife." He fell into step beside me.

I stiffened but didn't look at him. My stomach flipped and swished like a minnow in a pool. I would've darted back in the lodge and hid if I could. But I hardened my spine. I had never cowered before the warriors and never would.

A few more steps and a shadow moved out from behind a tree. Fenrir. Of course. Wherever Jarl was, Fenrir was not far behind and vice versa.

"Fine morning for a walk," Jarl said, as if I wasn't ignoring him. I shook my head and he winked at me.

I quickened my step, but his long legs barely had to stretch to keep up. "You no longer wear a veil," Jarl observed.

I touched my hair where once I would've worn a veil—a sign of my dedication to God. I'd given up wearing it after a few days on the mountain. I was no longer Sister Juliet.

I didn't know who I was anymore.

It was a beautiful day, if I ignored the presence of the two warriors who insisted on escorting me. At the abbey, my life had been divided into simple sections, bound by the bells. Prayer, work, meals, and more prayer. Sometimes there was fasting, sometimes feasts, though celebrations were mostly enjoyed by the village and rarely touched the abbey. My life inside the stone walls was simple, safe.

Now I lived on Berserker mountain. There were no bells to signal the passing hours. Only crickets and bird song. No neatly tended gardens. Only wildflowers and rugged pine. No rules, no prayers, no veil to bind my hair. Only a stunning view from the heights, and above, a vast unbroken sky.

But if God made the world, He made this land. Man tried to make the world small. Men built the abbey and bound the hours of the day to the bells. Men told me when I should rise, what I should eat, how I should work and dress.

How many of the rules I followed were not made by God, but made by men?

"You're upset," Jarl said.

I smoothed my forehead and shook my head.

When I reached the stream, Jarl didn't ask, he simply plucked the bucket from my hand and filled it from the stream. Fenrir came and took the other. I stood awkwardly on the bank, unable to ignore them any longer.

They were big as boulders, these warriors. Fenrir's black hair was unbound. It fell straight down his back, long enough dip into the water. Jarl had bound his hair back with a thong. They both wore leather breeches. Under a fur cape, Fenrir was bare-chested while Jarl had a sleeveless jerkin. Jarl's arms were covered with pagan symbols.

I reached for the water bucket as he returned to me, but he shook his head. I pivoted, woodenly, and started walking back to the lodge. I would take my time returning if I were alone, but I had no desire to linger with these men.

But I'd promised Meadow I'd ask them if we could visit Laurel. "I heard one of the spaewives is with child," I used the term the warriors preferred. *Spaewife* was a woman who could mate with a Berserker. "May we go visit her?"

"Which one?" Jarl responded, and my steps slowed.

"There's more than one with child?" Laurel, Hazel, Willow, and Sage were all settled with warriors. They'd been stolen from the abbey but seemed happy. All but Hazel were mated to not one, but two warriors. I couldn't imagine how that was possible.

I *shouldn't* imagine how that was possible. But after several moons with Jarl and Fenrir always near, I *had* imagined it.

God forgive me.

Jarl grinned as if he knew my thoughts. "Yes. Come spring, there'll be a new crop of babies."

Fenrir spoke up. "There's to be a feast four nights from now. In celebration."

I hid a sigh. "Perhaps we could go for the day and help with the preparation." Meadow and the rest would be in ecstasy. Rosalind hated leaving the lodge and would sulk for days.

"That can be arranged," Jarl said.

"Juliet." Fenrir flowed to my side, frowning. "Where are your boots?"

"I gave them to another girl." All the girls had grown since coming to the Berserker's mountain. Here we had food every day, and often it was meat. I could not fault the warriors for that. Little Clover and Aspen's eyes were bright and their cheeks rosy. Juniper had grown a foot in less than two moons. I'd given my boots to her.

Jarl tsked. "We would give you what you need. You've only to ask."

"I wouldn't dream of disturbing you with such a request. Surely you have more important things to do."

"Nothing as important as seeing to you."

Jarl moved in front of me on the path. I halted before I slammed into him. To my surprise, he knelt and set the bucket aside. His hand closed around my ankle and tugged. I went off balance and would've landed on my behind if Fenrir hadn't caught me in his arms.

"What are you doing?" I squawked.

Jarl frowned as he examined my feet. "You need to wear your boots. It's not summer anymore."

"Don't touch me," I snapped.

"You care so much for others, Juliet. But who will care for you?"

He let me go and Fenrir helped me to my feet. I moved away, clutching my cloak around myself as if that would protect me.

"Calm yourself," Jarl had the audacity to chuckle. I clenched my fist to keep from slapping him. "You have nothing to fear."

"No?" I rounded on him, snarling. "Then tell me, what is the purpose of holding us? Why did you bring us here to this mountain?" I knew the answer, of course, but all the anger I'd felt since that night in the abbey bubbled over.

"We seek women who can break our Berserker curse. You know this. Without a mate, we will go mad."

"And if we do not wish to be mates?"

Jarl cocked his head to the side. His gaze roamed up and down my form, and heat filled me, unbidden. "Give us a chance, little wife. You will be wanting and willing in no time."

I drew on my rage and let it armor me.

"You invaded our home and took us for brides," I snapped. "Some of these girls are no older than eight or nine summers. You would join them with warriors thrice their age?"

"There are many places where this is the custom," he chided, and I flushed. I knew that was true. I'd lived all my life in the abbey, but I knew the ways of the world.

"They are so young."

"Never fear, Juliet. The young ones are safe. You are safe." He drew close. If I wanted, I could reach out and touch him. Trace the lines of his tattoos up his arms, and see how much skin they covered.

I locked my hands under my arms. I'd vowed to remain

chaste and pure. Why, oh why did my palms ache to touch him?

"We wait until the spaewife is in heat," Fenrir explained. "Then the warriors will be allowed to court her."

"In heat?" I wrinkled my nose, unsure what he meant.

Jarl grinned and started to answer, but Fenrir cut him off. "The heat comes when the spaewife is ready to mate."

"And if the spaewife is never ready?" I asked quickly.

"Then she need not fear." Fenrir shrugged. "No warrior will touch a spaewife without permission. On pain of death. The Alphas have decreed it."

I blinked and all my ire left in a rush. "Well, then, that is good." The spaewives had told me this before, but I doubted them. Hearing Jarl and Fenrir confirm the Alphas' decree calmed me.

"Is that all you wish to rant about, little wife?" Jarl's eyes sparkled. "Or do you still wish to do battle?"

"Why do you call me wife? I am not a wife and never will be."

"No?" Gold flared in Jarl's eyes. He raised his head and sniffed the air in a smooth movement that reminded me of an animal. A wolf on the hunt.

My stomach fluttered and I smoothed my hands over my dress.

"I have a question," Fenrir said. He rarely talked, but his deep voice commanded attention.

I turned to him. "Ask."

Out of the corner of my eye, Jarl's jaw hardened. I took perverse pleasure ignoring him in favor of the taller warrior.

Fenrir sat on a rock so he no longer loomed over me. "Why do so many of the orphan girls bear names for trees and flowers?"

Finally, an easy question. "Some girls came to the abbey

as babes, with no names. The nuns named them. Sister Theresa named the first few for herbs, and the others followed convention."

Fenrir nodded, his face solemn as if I'd spoken a great secret. His gravitas encouraged me to sit on a nearby rock and explain further. "In the case of Rosalind and her sister, Rosalind had a name, and Aspen did not. She was too young."

"And your name is Juliet," Jarl butted in.

"Yes." I became very absorbed in picking a few flowers, the last blooms of mountain rue.

"So you knew your family," Jarl persisted.

"No. I was still too young. But I was old enough to be delivered with a name." I tossed the yellow flowers aside.

"Why did—" Jarl started to ask, and Fenrir cut him off with a mere shake of his dark head. Jarl subsided into silence with a muted snarl.

Strangely, it did not feel wrong to sit here in the morning light in the company of these Berserkers. Fenrir leaned down and snapped off a long stemmed daisy. He presented it to me and I took it, bringing it to my lips to hide my smile. I could feel Jarl tensing up, ready to explode.

"Fenrir," I said. "That means "wolf."

The 'wolf' in question dipped his head. I hesitated. These warriors, impossibly, were also wolves. And they had a third form, a monstrous shape I'd seen only a few times and at a distance, lurking in the woods. I wanted to ask after the Berserker curse, but couldn't bring myself to. If the friar were here, he'd decry these men as demons.

I shouldn't be curious. I should cross myself and try to pray.

Instead, I felt no fear, no dread of demons or hellfire.

Only curiosity and the desire to run my hands through Fenrir's long hair.

"Jarl's mother chose his name against his father's wishes," Fenrir said. His voice was light, teasing, and he gave a rare smile. "Perhaps, if you ask nicely, he will tell you why."

"Why?" I asked Jarl, who was glaring at Fenrir. The long-haired man laughed softly.

Jarl cleared his throat. "She thought I would become a *jarl*. An earl," he translated the word into my tongue. "A lord among men."

"Were you an earl's son, then?" I asked, confused.

Jarl cursed and Fenrir laughed outright.

"You are wise, little mother," Fenrir told me. Giddiness spread through me at his soft praise and heated gaze.

"Juliet," a girl's voice called, and I cursed under my breath. Meadow and Fern stood in the door of the lodge. Meadow shaded her eyes, looking for me. I jumped to my feet before they could see me seated and conversing with these men.

"I must go." Once again, I reached for the buckets but Fenrir beat me to it. I drew back before our hands could touch.

"Are you frightened of us?" he asked, lifting both buckets.

"No," I said without thinking. And it was true. I knew then they would not hurt me. I'd always known.

Fenrir's eyes lit in triumph. I stood facing them, scrubbing my hands over my dress. Something between us had shifted, and I knew not what. Or perhaps I didn't want to know.

"Go then, little mother." Fenrir handed me the buckets and nodded for me to return to the lodge. "Tell the unmated spaewives to prepare for a feast in a few day's time. Later, we will bring you the day's meal."

"Very well. Thank you. And...don't call me that." I hurried off, wondering if I'd made a fool of myself.

※

Fenrir

I watched the little nun hurry across the fields. She met her friends, two unmated spaewives younger than her. They embraced her and went back inside the lodge.

"She's coming into heat," Jarl muttered. "She hopes to hide it. But I caught the scent."

"She can't hide from us."

Down at the lodge, a throng of young girls tromped out, led by an older one. Juliet had a little one balanced on her hip. She did not glance at us as she ushered the girls along toward a flower-filled meadow in the other direction.

I crouched and touched the flowers Juliet had plucked and discarded. "She will resist, brother," I said.

Jarl's lip curled. "Easily overcome."

"And what about the Alphas' decree?"

"What about them?" he shrugged. "The Alphas say what they must, but when they found a spaewife they wanted for themselves, they did not hesitate to claim her."

"It's not the Alphas I'm concerned about. Their mates are protective of the unmated spaewives, especially the younger ones."

"Juliet is not young. She is old enough to feel her desires."

"And reject them."

Jarl glanced at the sky. "In four night's time, at the feast. There will be a full moon, and she will be in heat. We can make our desires known."

I let the broken petals filter through my fingers and fall to the ground. "Juliet is smart. She knows what we desire. She desires the same. The question is, will she accept it?"

3

Juliet

Four nights later, we all gathered on the other side of the mountain for the feast. As night crept over the fields, the full moon hung low in the sky, big and round and golden.

"Harvest moon," Sage said, traipsing from Laurel's large hearth to the great bonfire nestled down the hill.

"Hunter's moon," Hazel corrected and set a platter of shiny braided bread down on a rough hewn plank that acted as a table.

"Honey Moon," Laurel said without thinking and flushed when her friends giggled. Her figure was as lush as ever, her belly starting to curve under her full breasts.

I smiled at her and the others. I was older than these four, but we'd grown up together in the orphanage. They were the only sisters I'd known. "I hear that we will expect more than one babe after winter. Laurel's is one, but who is the other?"

As one, Sage, Hazel, and Willow put hands over their flat bellies. Then their eyes grew wide as they looked around at each other.

"You, Hazel?" Willow cried, at the same time Sage said, "You two, Willow?"

"And Sage also," Hazel announced. The three young women burst into squeals and started hugging one another.

"Oh. Oh my." Fat tears rolled down Laurel's face, even though her cheeks curved into a smile. "I'm happy, truly," she waved us off when we'd comfort her.

My breath was sharp enough to cut my chest. "Congratulations." I busied myself organizing the platters to make room for the meat. The Berserkers preferred to eat outside by the fires. Indeed, their main source of fun was building the bonfire as high as possible. Twice I'd had to warn the young girls back from the blaze. I'd brought a few blankets and spread them over the grass for us all to sit. Meadow, Angelica, and Fern were there now, keeping the little ones from running and getting underfoot.

Laurel was still crying. A huge warrior whose face was a mass of scars came up behind her. He bent and whispered in her ear, and pulled her close. She sighed and reached up to cup his neck as she leaned back on him. They made a lovely picture, the huge warrior cradling his curvy, pregnant bride.

I'll never have that, I thought. When I made my vows, they came easily. I did not want to leave the abbey and marry a man of the friar's choosing. I would be a nun. I would live my whole life in the shelter of the stone walls. I would be safe. I would live a life of my choosing. I loved children, but I could help in the orphanage and be surrounded by them without having them on my own.

The only thing I really had to give up was a future husband, and that was easy. What use did I have for a man? And if some nights I went to bed aching with loneliness, well, at least I would not have to submit to any man. Only God. I could conquer my own desires.

But that was before I met the Berserkers.

I finished with the food and trekked back to my own group. The unmated spaewives, as the Berserkers called us. But even among them, I didn't belong.

"Juliet," Meadow waved at me and made room on the blanket for me to sit. The sun was sinking, but there was still enough light for games. A group of warriors played a violent game of some sort, dashing and darting, trying to catch a leather bound ball. Of course, the Berserkers played half naked. Only a scrap of leather covered their nethers.

Some of the men didn't even have that.

Meadow's eyes were huge. I resisted the urge to put my hands over her eyes, and scrubbed my own instead. Sleepless nights and smoke from the massive bonfire made my head ache.

But it was more than that. Deep in my belly, I felt it brewing. The heat, rising in me. It had come on me before, but it was worse tonight than it'd ever been.

Sage and Willow called it *the fever*. They and many of our sisters had felt it. From what they told me, the heat called to the Berserkers. It marked the women who could break their curse.

And now it had come upon me.

"The heat comes when the spaewife is ready to mate." Fenrir had told me. I put a hand to my belly and gnawed my lip.

Maybe I was a spaewife. Or maybe I was just wicked, and destined to burn. This sickness was the heat of hellfire, warning me to renounce all sin.

A half-naked warrior strolled past me and Meadow gasped. On her corner of the blanket, Fern ducked her head to her knees, though she peeked out from time to time.

Rosalind sat on a boulder some feet away from us. She sat straight and stiff, her honey gold hair streaming out behind her like a flag. Half the warriors blatantly stared at her. A few even tried to catch her attention. But she stared out at nothing, proud as a princess, refusing to acknowledge her captors.

"Look," Meadow nudged me. "The Alphas are here."

And so they were, taking their place on a crop of boulders nearer to the fire. Their women came with them, Brenna of the Berserkers, dark-haired and lovely in a white fur robe that trailed upon the grass. Sabine of the Lowland pack, tall and flanked by two warriors—one of whom had more tattoos than Jarl. Muriel and her hulking, scar-faced mate. A fourth slender, bright-haired woman who held a staff taller than her head. When she strode past us amid a tight pack of three warriors, I noticed the wood staff was carved with runes and topped with an eagle feather.

The Alphas settled and the feasting began. As the warriors carved up the game, I found myself looking for a certain two Berserkers. But Jarl and Fenrir weren't among the warriors.

By the time the moon rose, we'd eaten our fill of the meat and sprawled out, half on the blanket, half on the grass. The younger ones dozed. I'd taken off my cloak to make a pillow for Aspen, Ivy, and Clover.

Down by the fire, the Alphas still ate and drank. A few Berserkers rolled up huge casks of mead. When the first opened, the honey liquid spilled to the ground and the warriors sent up a cheer.

That's when I saw him, standing among his Berserker pack. Fenrir stood near the casks, sipping from a cup. A minute later Jarl joined him.

I knew I shouldn't stare, but I couldn't help it. They bent toward one another, then Fenrir's head snapped up as if he suddenly sensed something. Before I could look away, he turned and looked straight at me.

I squirmed in my seat. Jarl looked up at me, too. His usual smirk spread across his face and he raised his horn of mead in a mock toast to me.

I looked away. I didn't know why I'd sought them out in the first place. They didn't matter to me. I needed to remember that.

Night had fallen. The bonfire had grown bigger, fed by whole trees. A single Berserker could fell a tree in seconds and carry it on their own. It seemed to be a competition among them, second only to competing to see who could drink a whole cask of mead.

I sighed and hugged my knees to my chest. Soon our warrior guard would come and escort us back to our beds. But for now, we would sit and watch the wild revelry. It was a welcome change from the stuffy lodge.

Then the drums began. First, a subtle throbbing, echoing over the hill. I did not know whence it came. The sound grew into a low pulse that seemed to shake the very ground from deep inside. The heartbeat of the earth.

A group of people wearing cloaks were coming up the hill toward our gathering. They pushed back their hoods as they entered the circle of the bonfire's light. Most were women, but not any I recognized. Some were old and bent, others had smooth, ageless faces. One tall woman carried a huge snowy owl on her outstretched arm.

They were witches, I realized. The Alphas rose as one to greet them.

The rhythm of the drums intensified.

The newcomers settled into their own circle, some ways from the Alphas. The Berserkers were gathering in a larger circle around the witches and the whole bonfire. The firelight danced and licked over blonde heads and gleaming torcs, over axe heads and shields. The warrior's dark tattoos seemed to come alive, the symbols writhing over the warriors' skin.

A ripple went through the gathered warriors. Sabine walked from the Alphas' seat toward the witches, accompanied by her two mates. When she reached the witches' circle, she let her cloak fall away. She'd been painted with woad, her face and bare arms covered in blue symbols. She wore a white shift and nothing else. Her feet were bare.

The drums beat faster. The witch with the owl greeted Sabine, and raised her voice to the assembly. I couldn't hear anything over the boom of the drums. Or maybe I didn't want to hear.

I licked my lips. Behind me, the younger girls had fallen asleep, lulled by the pagan rhythms. Rosalind was standing now, her face a pale mask bathed in moonlight. Beside me, Fern curled tighter into a ball, rocking slightly.

In the circle of witches, Sabine began to dance. She twisted and turned, her bare feet striking the earth, her body dipping and flowing like a willow's branches. At times, she raised her face and arms to the moon and the drums would pause, only to continue faster.

The rhythms built and built, and as one, the Berserkers

raised their weapons to the sky. The witches sent up a chant and the Berserkers echoed it. They beat their axes and swords against their shields, adding to the rhythm of the drums.

A warrior entered the circle with Sabine. Ragnvald, one of the Alphas and one of her mates. He moved to her side. In a flash, he reached out and caught her, and drew her close with a fist in her bright hair. She stilled, rising on tiptoe to face him, her hands hanging by her sides, palms out turned.

The warrior Ragnvald held Sabine fast. His face moved over hers, hovering as he scented along her hairline. Even from my distance, I could see her eyes close. She quivered in his grip.

Slowly Ragnvald dipped his head and claimed her mouth. All the Berserker warriors broke into a war cry, shaking their weapons.

I jerked at the clamor and looked around. Hazel sat watching the ritual beside a giant golden-haired warrior. A few feet away, higher on the hill, Willow sat between two warriors, one dark, one redhead. As I watched, the redhead cupped her face and kissed her.

I gasped, a flush moving over me. A second went by, and another, but the kiss between Willow and her mate did not end. Beyond them, Laurel lay between her mates. Their large hands stroked back her hair and along the curve of her bosom.

I rose to my feet, a wave of heat pulsing over me. Hazel was now in her warrior's lap, her small dress-clad frame dwarfed by his. Her warrior giant played with the torc around her neck, tugging it to draw her closer and lying back so she could straddle him.

I whirled to face the woods, my face burning. It was suddenly too hot. My nails scraped my chest as if I could peel out of my skin. My heartbeat boomed loud as the drums.

"Juliet?" It was Fern, concern in her voice. I shook my head at her and tried to speak, but the drums filled my ears.

The drums were driving me mad. I was nowhere near the bonfire, but my skin burned like I was in the middle of its molten mouth. Sweat dripped into my eyes and my eyes blurred.

I had to escape. There must be somewhere, anywhere I could hide.

I turned and raced toward the woods. The ground seemed to roll under my feet as I reached the treeline. I wore new boots; boots I'd found by the lodge three nights ago. They were welcome then, but now seemed too heavy on my feet.

I stumbled.

"Juliet." Fenrir stepped out from behind a tree and caught me as I fell. I was in his arms, surrounded by his scent. His long hair swept over me. I pushed at the fine tangle until our faces were clear.

And then his mouth was on mine. His dark beard scratched my face. His hands cupped my jaw, turning my head this way and that as his tongue plundered. My arms went around his broad shoulders, gripping handfuls of his silky hair. Our bodies melded to each other. My aching breasts brushed his smooth chest.

His mouth broke from mine. We were both gasping. He propped me against a tree trunk. My hair caught on the rough bark.

Then Jarl was before me, shouldering Fenrir out of the

way. He gripped my hair, hard. I gasped. He tugged my head back and sealed my lips with a brutal kiss. His mouth blazed a path down my neck. His teeth tested and gently bit my collarbone. He drew me away from the tree and Fenrir closed in again. Using my hair as a leash, Jarl turned my face to Fenrir's for another soft kiss. Then back to his for a claiming one. Back and forth while the moon rose and the drumbeat throbbed between my legs. In a moment, they would drag me down and we'd tangle together on the ground. It would be so easy.

I wrenched away. Jarl growled, but Fenrir stopped him from jerking me back. I stumbled a few paces and both warriors let me.

"No," I said, too soft for any man to hear. "I cannot."

"Juliet," Fenrir called.

I faced them with chin raised. "I have given my life to God."

"A nun. We know."

"Then you know that I am chaste."

"You are not chaste." Jarl stepped close. I retreated from him, only to stop when my back hit a tree. The tip of his mouth curled upwards and his rough hand covered my breast. "You desire us. You always will." He leaned close and his lips feathered up my neck.

I was panting as if I'd run up the mountain. "You know me not at all."

"Give us time. We will know every part of you." Jarl whispered into my ear. I could hear his smirk.

I dashed his hands away. Jarl stepped back, chuckling.

Fenrir came close then, his hands outspread. "Juliet." Moonlight filtered across his face, gilding his beautiful features. Desire shot through me.

I averted my face.

"Juliet, look at me." His palm cupped my cheek. It felt so good I shuddered.

"You cannot touch me." I told him. "I've dedicated my life to God."

"Which God?" Jarl asked.

I frowned at him. "There is only one true God."

Jarl shrugged. "We have many." He leaned against the tree, close to me. "Perhaps that is why your prayers don't work. For me, if one god is deaf, I pray to another."

"That is blasphemy," I whispered. What was I doing, facing these men alone? I ducked past Fenrir and shouted over my shoulder, "Do not come near me again."

I was shaking when I returned to my group. Fern looked at me worriedly. I gathered a slumbering Clover onto my lap and fixed my eyes on the fire. I paid no attention when Jarl and Fenrir joined the rest of the warriors. They were nothing to me. I would never speak to them again. I would remain at the lodge and pray for my heat to pass.

Surely, God would answer my prayers and drive the lust from my flesh, and when that happened, the fever would leave.

∼

BUT THE FEVER did not leave. As seasons past and autumn gave way to winter, I grew to dread the full moon. My heat did not pass. It grew worse.

And finally came the night when I sat shivering in frozen mud. The Berserkers had watched and waited, and now their patience was at an end.

"This ends now," Fenrir said, and my heart beat like a war drum.

Jarl and Fenrir would allow me to resist no longer. They would claim me, and my suffering would be over.

It would only come at the cost of my vows, and my pride.

The warriors surrounded me, caging me between them. There was no escape.

Jarl bent his head to mine. "We're taking you this night."

And deep down, I felt relief.

4

Jarl

THE LITTLE NUN shrank into herself. She didn't fight other than try to tug her arm away. It took a mere fraction of my strength to hold her. She gave up and blinked at me. Her pale skin glowed in the moonlight, and her pulse fluttered in her throat.

I dipped my head down to whisper in the silken shell of her ear.

"You're suffering. You've been suffering so long you know no other life. But we can end it. You refuse to, so we will. We won't stand by and watch any longer."

"You can't do this," she whispered back.

"We're Berserkers," I taunted back. "We'll do as we wish."

Her eyes flashed and I straightened, smirking. The Juliet

I knew would not cower before us. She'd fight back. Even frightened, she'd fight.

Jarl, Fenrir spoke into my mind, through the mental bond all Berserkers shared. *The changing of the guard is soon. We best be gone.*

"Come, little mother." I caught her up in my arms, and strode away from the lodge. Fenrir followed.

Juliet's breathing grew sharp. I splayed a hand on her back to calm her, and picked up my speed. We flew into the forest. I cradled her close as I pushed through the thicket of hemlock branches. Juliet hid her face against my shoulder. Poor little spaewife.

"What about the girls?" she muttered.

"They will be safe," Fenrir promised. "The spaewives will watch over them."

"But—"

"Hush," I murmured. "You think always of others, never of yourself."

Juliet tried to wrench herself away from me. When I would not let her, she pressed her lips together and glared up at me. If her gaze was an axe, it'd separate me from my head.

I grinned. "No matter, little mother. We will take care of you."

When I broke from the trees, I linked to Fenrir, speaking mind to mind. *She's cold.*

Fenrir shrugged out of the fur robe he wore. It left his chest bare, but he was a Berserker. The magic that made us allowed us to ignore the cold.

When Fenrir approached to drape the fur on Juliet, she roused.

"No." Juliet's teeth chattered as she tried to talk. "You'll freeze."

"Hush, little mother," I cupped the back of her head, trying to ease her back against my chest.

"I won't freeze," Fenrir told her. "I'm a Berserker."

Her brow creased, but she stopped fighting. We bundled her into the fur. She'd need it, as we crossed to the north side of the mountain. Branches and frosted grass crunched underfoot. Fenrir moved silently beside me. I could glide quietly as a wolf, but we wanted to leave a trail.

When we came to a stream, we waded right in. I gritted my teeth against the numbing cold. An ordinary man would freeze, but the magic that healed us would stop any frostbite. Fenrir and I agreed to walk the stream to throw off our scent. It would not stop the Alphas from tracking us, but it would delay them a little.

After a mile walking in the water, we came to the cliff where we'd built our lodge. The moonlight shone down on the lodge roof in silent blessing. We were on the other side of the mountain. Most Berserkers would not bring their mates so far from the safety of the pack, but we had no choice. Not if we were to claim her.

Juliet was quiet, her breathing even. For a moment I thought she'd fallen asleep. Perhaps this would be easier than I thought.

Then she raised her head.

She was still shuddering, her small frame wracked with cold.

"Where are you taking me?" she asked.

"To our home." I couldn't keep the pride from my voice. We'd built this place for our mate, and now we were bringing her home.

She sucked in a breath and blew it out in a frosty cloud. "This is a mistake. You shouldn't have taken me."

There were a few large boulders in our path. I maneuvered around them and picked up my pace, climbing up the rise toward the lodge. "Why didn't you scream for help?"

"I didn't want to disturb the girls. They've been through so much."

"They are safe now."

She snorted. "Safe," she sneered.

"They are safe," I repeated.

"They are my responsibility," she said. "I don't trust the Berserkers."

"We protect them. They are spaewives."

"Until they are of age to be brides?" she asked sharply. I loved that I held her in my arms and yet she wanted to argue with me.

"They are spaewives." I adjusted her closer. "Do you want them to suffer the fever, as you have?"

"No." She bit her lip and looked tormented. Another shiver ran through her.

Fenrir eased into a stride beside me. He reached over to adjust the fur to cover Juliet more fully, then took her hand. "Do not worry for them. They have their own path. You have yours."

"And my path leads straight to your lodge?" She glowered at Fenrir, but I noticed she did not pull her hand away.

I hitched her higher in my arms and their handhold broke. Maybe I did it on purpose, maybe it was a mistake.

The path curved around another crop of boulders. Instead of following it, I leapt up, holding her tight in my arms. She gasped and clung to me.

"Look down there," I ordered. She did and squinted into the dark. I paced a little closer to the edge of the lichen covered rock.

Jarl, Fenrir said my name in warning, speaking into my mind.

It's safe. She must see.

For a moment Juliet did nothing but squint into the dark. Then her body stiffened, and I knew what she saw—the magical boundary that ended at the foot of the cliff. The edge of the barrier that enclosed and protected the mountain. On one side, snow bitten rocks and grasses quivered in the wind. On the other, the ground was bare, trampled to mud by foul feet. The monstrous *draugr* marched along the boundary, at times pausing to press their rotting corpse bodies against the magical barrier and howl. The wind carried their moans away.

"See what we protect you from?" I asked quietly. I didn't want to scare her, but this was necessary. She had to know.

She gulped. "What are they?"

"The Corpse King's creatures. He is a mage of old. He seeks spaewives to marry so he can steal their magic."

She shook her head, still staring at the undead horde.

"This is what we saved you from. This is why we took you from the abbey."

"Jarl," Fenrir warned. *You're upsetting her.*

She is already upset. She thinks us monsters? Let us show her what monsters truly are.

Her trembling increased, and I couldn't take it anymore. I leapt down to the path and started climbing again with long strides. "Come. We've lingered too long in the cold."

∽

Juliet

. . .

Inside the lodge, the scent of sawdust bit my nose. I sneezed just as Jarl set me down. He held on to me, and I pushed him away, sneezing again. I did not want his help.

"Juliet," he murmured, but let me stagger away from him. I was no longer freezing—Fenrir's fur robe had warmed me, and even though the air inside the lodge was not warmer, it was at least sheltered from the wind.

I turned in a slow circle, examining the place they'd brought me. This lodge was not unlike the lodge of the unmated spaewives.

They'd kidnapped me from my home now twice. First from the abbey, then from the lodge where they'd promised I'd be safe. They'd stripped me of everything I'd known.

All I had left were my vows, and even those they would leave in tatters.

I walked further into the lodge, aware of two large shadows stalking me. Jarl and Fenrir. The warriors who'd dragged me from the abbey, my home. Who sheltered and protected me.

I ignored them to explore the place they'd brought me to. There was a fire pit near the entrance. Stacks of wood and a few barrels lined the walls. At the back was a frame for stretching and drying furs.

In the middle of the lodge was a huge bed. Whole trees had been hewn to make it. It was piled high with furs.

I reached out and rubbed the polished wood, then sank my hand in the silky furs.

"Will you take me this night?" My voice was oddly detached. It would take nothing for them to strip me and lay me down on the bed, and claim me as I knew they wanted to.

What was worse, deep down, a part of me wanted them to.

Kyrie eleison. Christos eleison. Lord have mercy. Christ have mercy.

They'd brought me here to break my vows. If not this night, then soon.

I turned and faced them. They towered over me.

The warriors exchanged a look. I knew they communicated mind to mind, another form of sorcery I should renounce, but I was too tired.

"No," Jarl answered. "Not this night, but soon."

"Does he always speak for you?" I baited Fenrir. Perverse of me to pick at the silent Berserker, but perhaps I could turn him against Jarl. I needed every weapon I could gain.

"No," Fenrir answered, and ambled out of the lodge.

"Where is he going?" I rubbed my arms under the fur Fenrir had given me.

Jarl tugged me close and rubbed my arms over the fur, chafing them until warmth rose. "He goes to fetch wood for a fire. Why did you poke at him? Were you trying to pick a fight?"

I flushed. Was I that transparent?

"Surely you must fight with him sometimes."

Jarl shrugged. "Often. But he has been my brother for over a hundred years."

I pulled away. "What is the magic that binds you? Is it evil?"

"You've seen us fight." He crouched in the middle of the lodge to strike a blaze in the sooty pit. His muscles flexed and his eyes blazed gold. "You've seen us at rest. What do you think?"

"The abbess would say it is pagan magic."

"Is all pagan magic evil?" He had a small fire going, and cupped his hands around it to protect it from the draft. His hands and face glowed like a demon's.

"Yes," I said, but my tone was unsure.

He looked up at me then. "Always?"

I raised my chin. "That was what I was taught."

Slowly he rose, unfolding to his great height, towering over me. "And everything you were taught is true?"

With that troubling question, he left the lodge and I was alone. The fire crackled at my feet. Soon Jarl and Fenrir would return with kindling for it, but right now I could sneak out. This might be my only chance.

I ran to the back of the lodge. It was sturdily constructed, the boards so new, the wood hadn't faded. It was bright and sawdust colored, with a few beads of sap dried mid-drip on the light surface.

There had to be a way out. There—in the corner. A narrow entrance that could easily be covered by a tapestry. A second exit along the back of the lodge.

I raced and would've stepped out, but before I could dart through it, a shadow moved in the darkness beyond. I shrank back, hand on my heart. Was it a wild animal moving outside the lodge?

Then the dark shape bent to duck inside the door. When it straightened, I recognized Fenrir. He'd caught me.

Silently, Fenrir moved inside the lodge, crowding me back toward the fire. There was a bundle of kindling under his arm.

I stared at the center of his bare chest. His skin was darker than mine and even Jarl's, and not only from the sun. He was smooth, too, his muscles sleek without the mat of hair most men had.

I swallowed.

His finger came to my jaw. He traced up, a light touch, but enough to set my nerves simmering. "Do not leave," he spoke in his deep voice. "It's not safe, little mother."

I frowned, still staring at the center of his chest. "Why do you call me that?"

"Little mother? Because you are little."

"I'm not a mother."

"Aren't you?"

"No. I have remained chaste. I haven't borne a child."

"Tell that to the younglings in the spaewife lodge. You mother them all." He moved past me, and knelt to feed the sticks he'd brought to the fire.

I inched away toward the back of the lodge again. I'd missed this chance to escape, but maybe another would come.

Then the front door blasted open and Jarl came in stamping. "Getting colder. Too cold for spring. Another blizzard's coming. The Corpse King wreaking his will on the weather."

I tried not to shiver. And failed because Jarl immediately looked to me.

"Come near the fire, Juliet."

I shook my head, wrapping my arms more tightly around me.

"Do not make me fetch you," Jarl said. Fenrir's head dropped to his chest, but he didn't quite hide his grin.

I shifted on either foot. Jarl dropped the logs he carried and started in my direction, and I scurried to the other side of the fire, hating myself for giving in.

I bared my teeth at Jarl like I was a wolf.

"Is this the way it will be? Do you have to lord your will over me every moment?"

He set his jaw. "I told you I would not let you suffer."

"I suffer in your presence," I shot back.

"As long as you are not cold." He smirked and went back

to tending the fire. Soon the flames were higher than my head.

I hovered at the side of the lodge, gritting my teeth against the drafts that went up my dress. The lodge was well-built, but along the wall there were cracks that let in some cold. Nothing a good blaze couldn't drive out.

I tried to stay away but the warmth and light beckoned me closer. Much as I hated it, Jarl was right. My legs were numb. I could not stay away from their fire forever.

I sat on a fur covered rock set close to the fire. It was strange to sit and rest while there was work to be done, but I was a captive here. I would not stir myself to help lest these warriors think I was content in my captivity.

Fenrir and Jarl moved with purpose, and for the first time I let myself watch them. They both were huge but light on their feet, their movements fluid and graceful as a pair of deer. Or more accurately, a pair of wolves. Jarl spoke the most and I thought of him as their leader, but when they were silent and moving in unspoken concert, they were equal. Fenrir was slightly taller with long dark hair flowing down his back. If he were one of the young women in my charge, I'd make him sit so I could braid it. He was more beautiful, with a narrow face and long dark eye lashes.

Jarl was stockier and broad in the shoulder, though he was tall enough, certainly taller than me. His face was broad, and he'd be handsome if he wasn't always smirking at me.

Among all the Berserkers, I'd always noticed them. What was amazing was that they'd noticed me.

"Juliet." Jarl was standing beyond the fire. My gaze snapped to his, and I blushed. He'd caught me looking. No wonder he was smirking.

Maybe all the times I'd snuck a look, I hadn't hidden it as well as I'd thought.

I wrapped my arms around my legs.

"What is this place?"

"This is the place we built for you."

"Me? Why?"

"Because you're our mate."

"I am no one's mate."

"Because of your vows?"

My brow prickled with sweat and I wiped it away. The walk had cooled me, but now the fire made me hot again. Or maybe I was still feverish.

"You can't eat, you can't sleep. We've watched you suffer all these moons—"

"And what, you thought you'd steal me away and I would fall into your bed and it would all be fine?" I glared and he grinned. The angrier I got, the more I amused him and the more amused he became, the angrier I got.

"You will let us care for you." Fenrir settled next to me.

"I will?" I turned my glare to him but he remained calm.

"You will," he stated quietly, and offered me a water skin. I was thirsty, so I let him raise it to my lips and nodded when I'd had enough to drink. Then he opened a pack and handed me a strip of dried meat. I ate and when he leaned closer to me, I didn't stiffen and pull away. Fenrir's calm assurance had always steadied me. I didn't mind that he softened me. I preferred his company to Jarl's anyway.

"You have no choice," Jarl said from his place across the fire. Light and shadow played over his face as he watched us.

I stiffened and Fenrir sighed. He offered me more meat and I refused this time. But when I tried to turn away, he surprised me by pulling me into his lap.

"Calm yourself, little mother. Rest against me."

"I do not want this," I muttered. I was a grown woman sitting on a man's lap.

"Really? Then why does your body call to mine?" He reached around to lay a hand at my throat. His fingers half circled my neck and his palm rested over my breastbone. I wriggled and he pressed down lightly. I stop fidgeting. I couldn't escape, and it felt nice. "You're fighting it, little one." His deep voice caressed me. "There is no need."

Under his palm, my heartbeat fluttered and fought. His scent surrounded me, wild and rich, pine and wood smoke. I relaxed in his lap.

"We've never meant you any harm. We would do anything for you," he whispered into my ear.

"I only wish you to leave me alone," I said loud enough for Jarl to hear.

Fenrir's chuckle shook my whole body. "That is not true."

"It is true," I protested. His fingers tipped my head to the side and his beard brushed my neck. My body, caged and cradled by his, rose and fell as he breathed in my scent.

"You've been in heat all this time. Do not deny it."

Across the fire, Jarl watched, his eyes dark pits with the occasional flare of gold flame.

My own eyes grew heavy and my body relaxed, lulled by the warmth and comfort of the fire and Fenrir's lap. It was so nice to rest, cradled in a strong warrior's arms. Nothing in the world could hurt me here. Nothing.

His hand moved down, his fingertips brushing the tops of my breasts. My heart thudded loud enough to shake the lodge. Fenrir's lips were at my ear, and I strained to listen, but he said nothing. He nibbled along the outer edge and nipped the lobe. My body responded, tightening muscles deep in my core. I was a bud, tightly furled. A clenched fist, shaking with effort to remain closed.

His tongue touched the sensitive spot behind my ear, and a rush of golden feeling flooded me, rolling up from my core and spreading outwards in waves of tingling pleasure. It did not relieve the ache between my legs, but it edged the pain with sweetness, a promise of what was to come. All I had to do was let my legs fall open and accept what pleasure would come.

Fenrir's tongue traced along the edge of my ear, teasing each ridge. Each stroke of his tongue reverberated through my body, the golden waves growing in size and intensity.

Then he thrust his tongue into my ear.

I gasped and the sound seemed to echo through the lodge. Across the fire pit, Jarl leaned forward, almost into a crouch. His firelit form was as monstrous as the shadows he cast. Flame and shadow turned him into a demon ready to drag me to the pit of hell.

Fenrir's beard scraped my neck and ear. "Shhhh, little one." His large hand reaffirmed its gentle grip on my throat.

And then I realized what I'd been chanting, over and over. *Kyrie eleison, Christos eleison.* My chest was tight as if a boulder rested on it. Without my bidding, my lips moved to form the well-worn prayer.

Fenrir loosened his grip on me. He eased me up off his lap, slowly, but the blood rushed to my head. I swayed, unable to stand on my own. He steadied me with a hand on either arm.

"Be not afraid," he murmured. "Juliet, you're not harmed."

I jerked away. "That wasn't me." I pulled the fur around me tighter, as if it were armor against their gaze. I was shaking, but not with fear or anger. "You're making me someone I'm not."

Fenrir stepped close, moving slowly, deliberately. He approached as if I was a frightened rabbit, tensed to run. And maybe I was, but something rooted my feet to the ground.

He stopped when he stood before me, his body close enough for us to touch. One deep breath and my breasts would brush against him.

He lifted his hand, slowly, giving me enough time to pull away. My whole body held its breath, waiting for his touch, but he only stroked a tendril of hair away from my face. "You're who you've always been. You're the one who's denied it."

I opened my mouth, but I had no answer. Just the prayer I'd always prayed.

For years, I'd been praying long and hard. I'd built a wall between me and my desire, each prayer another stone. But tonight, the prayers were not enough to hold back the flood.

One touch from these warriors, and cracks formed in the wall. One kiss, and the dam would burst. All the feeling I had fought against would rush out and carry me away.

I waited with my face upturned, but no kiss came. Instead Fenrir dropped his hand and moved away.

"I'll take first watch," he told Jarl. He did not have to speak aloud to say this, so I knew he did so for my benefit. Then Fenrir left and I was alone with Jarl.

"He's right, you know. There's no use fighting. You want it too."

I couldn't resist Fenrir's tender touch, but Jarl's words pricked me, goaded me to fight. I drew the cloak around me like a shield and sneered at him. "I want nothing from you."

"So you say." He stood up and I startled back, but he made no move to approach me. "But is it true?"

I twisted my hands in the fur. "Of course it's true." But I was panting again. The fever was rising in me, no longer a golden wave but one tinged red. My core cramped, sending shockwaves of bloodred pain through my gut. I groaned and Jarl took a step toward me. But I stiffened, angling myself away from him, and he stopped.

"Juliet." He spread his hands to show me he held no weapon. "We mean you no harm."

"You've done enough." I shook in the grip of another cramp. My body had turned against me and I was helpless in its possession.

"Little one," his voice cracked. He quivered as if barely holding himself in check.

"Go, please. I can't do this. I can't fight you." I hung my head. I was so tired. Another minute and I'd slump to the floor.

"As you wish," he murmured. "The bed is there, ready for you."

It took all I had to drag myself there. The bed was made to hold a Berserker—or two. I had to jump and grab the heavy fur robes, scrambling to hoist myself up. And once up, I sank into the softness, lost in a sea of furs. Vast as the bed was, add two warriors and it'd be cozy and warm.

But I could not think of that.

I burrowed under the silky pile.

"Go to sleep, Juliet," Jarl said. He sounded tired, too. "We will speak more of this in the morning."

5

Juliet

I KNELT *on the flagstones before the altar. The stone bit my knees. I'd been kneeling for hours, but I'd kneel a hundred more. The church sanctuary was dark and stank of mold, but I'd always found comfort here. Before me on her pedestal, a statue of the Virgin Mother regarded me, a placid expression on the stone face. I'd often come to the sanctuary to hide from the cruel nuns and contemptuous friar. I look up at the statue and pretend I had a mother. She would be kind. She would care for me. She would never leave me as my own mother had. In my imagination, my mother's face looked like the Virgin Mother's, perfectly serene. Tonight, I imagined a touch of pity as I whispered my prayers.*

Kyrieeleisonchristoseleison. Pleasepleaseplease—

A knock sounded on the heavy wooden door. The whole sanctuary shook. I crouched lower and prayed faster. But the knock sounded again, and cracks ran down the flagstones. Above my head, the sanctuary roof cracked, letting in the light. Stones fell and dust rained down.

The voices of warriors rose and fell beyond the door. They were coming. They could not be stopped.

Please, I begged the Virgin Mother, but she was silent. The building shook and the door came down. Heavy footsteps sounded, but I could not turn or run. I was frozen like the statue, staring at the Virgin Mother face.

Tears poured from her eyes. Her small stone hand, raised in blessing, cracked and fell. I screamed as the entire statue crumbled.

My eyes snapped open. I lay in a cloud formed from the softest furs, suffocating in the heat. I clawed at the heavy robe, and the fur shifted, fell away. I felt it rumble something in sleep. I pushed at the solid fur wall, then jerked my hand away.

There was a large wolf on the bed. White with flecks of tawny brown.

I twisted and met another slumbering shape of dark fur.

Not one wolf, but two. Sleeping heavily as if enchanted.

I sat up slowly, but they didn't stir. We were in the large bed, in the new lodge Jarl and Fenrir had built.

In the hearth pit, the fire had died. Along the walls were stacks of firewood. And hung in the doorway was a dead deer. The warriors had spent the night working then, and gone on a hunt. No wonder they were tired.

Inch by inch, I left the blissful warmth and wriggled off the bed. Other than the odd twitching ear, the wolves didn't stir.

I bit my lip. Slowly I tugged the robe Fenrir had given me, freeing it from under the white wolf's paws. It was a heavy pelt. Not perfect, but it'd help fend off the cold.

This was my chance to escape. Maybe my last chance.

Outside the sky was slate grey. Snowflakes danced in the air, their fine white powder dusting the ground.

This was foolishness. I could not escape.

My bare toes curled, already stiff from the chilled ground. I would not last a journey in a snowstorm. Even the deer was already frozen, its blood congealed in a pool below its head.

I stared out at the frigid landscape, wishing I had wings to fly away.

Warmth hit my back a second before a tattooed arm curled around my chest. Jarl pulled me against him. His scent surrounded me—smoke and pine and another faint essence, like the smell of the air after a storm. Magic. The strange smell pricked my nose, fading as Jarl nuzzled the back of my neck with his bearded face.

"Come back to bed," he murmured against my skin.

I was panting as if I'd run up a mountain. "I cannot."

"You must. You are cold."

"No," I protested, but he was already drawing me backward. Somehow, he ended up before me and I turned my face away. Other than his dark tattoos and a piece of leather slung around his hips, he was naked. The cold nor my embarrassment didn't seem to bother him. He set me on the bed and knelt to examine my feet.

"Woman, you have no boots." His thumbs brushed the dirt and ash from the balls of my feet. My toes scrunched, first with the cold, then with pleasure as he massaged the tension out of me.

A strange wind lifted my hair, filling the lodge with the scent of rain. Then Fenrir was at my back, pulling me further onto the bed and into his arms. I tried to draw my legs in and roll away, but Fenrir squeezed me, gently but firm enough to hold me in place. At my feet, Jarl growled and gripped my feet. His strong hands massaged up my frozen calves.

"Please," I wriggled to face Fenrir. His long hair streamed over me, a black curtain. He was most assuredly naked too. I dared not look down. "We shouldn't lie like this, we can't—"

"Shhhh." He set a finger to my lips, then traced it over my brow. "There's a storm out there. We hunted last night, and there's plenty of wood. No reason to leave."

"I shouldn't be here." It was hard to argue when Jarl's fingers stroked magic up my legs. My thin shift was no barrier to either of them.

"Mmm," Fenrir didn't seem to hear. He was too intent on smoothing the line of my jaw, brushing back my hair.

I was drowning. Already my eyes were heavy, my body warm and sinking into the pleasurable, dreamlike sensations.

From faraway, I heard myself murmur, "I can't do this. I can't be what you want."

"You do not know what we want," Fenrir murmured. His thumb teased my lips. When I opened my mouth to speak, he slid a long finger inside, and then another. His two fingers invaded my mouth while I sucked, my eyes wide.

"Shhhh," he soothed. His two fingers stroked my tongue, and I felt the echo of their touch between my legs.

Meanwhile, warm breath curled over my ankle. Jarl gripped my feet, nibbling gently up my leg. My core contracted in anticipation and I closed my eyes. What was happening? Who was I?

A cold gust blew straight into the lodge, strong enough to send the deer swaying. Both warriors rose, cursing. Jarl went to secure the meat, and Fenrir followed, muttering something about needing a door and a fire.

And I lost all my sense.

Grabbing the nearest pelt, I scrambled off the bed, threw it around my shoulders, and dashed to the back of the lodge and out the door.

The cold hit me like a stone wall. I cried out and staggered, hissing as the cold sliced my skin. The frozen ground was like knives on my bare feet.

I'd gone no further than the edge of the clearing before shouts followed me.

"Juliet! Juliet!"

I crashed into the brush, mindless. I had no more wits than a frightened pheasant, flying up before the hunter. I half ran, half fell down the rise.

A white shape flew into my path and landed in front of me. I scrambled back from the white wolf blocking my path.

Then a strong arm clamped around my chest. "Got you," Jarl snarled. I struggled, but his arm tightened like an iron band. Then he tossed me up into his arms and ran back up the mountain.

Back in the lodge, the warmth smacked me in the face. Jarl plopped me on the bed again, but remained, gripping my shoulders.

"You little fool," he shook me. My teeth were already chattering, but my heart leaped in fear. "What were you thinking? Running out into a storm? With no boots?"

The white wolf slipped inside and barked.

"She needs to think," Jarl snapped at the wolf before turning back to me. "Is your god so cruel he would have you to die before you submit to us?"

I was sobbing, my chest tight with strain. This morning,

last night, the past few months all weighed on my understanding.

The wolf growled, its white fur standing on end. It stalked forward on stiff front legs, its teeth bared at the warrior.

"You talk to her, then," Jarl raged. And he stomped out of the lodge.

I crumpled on the bed, curling into a ball. My feet ached. My nose stung as if the tip had nearly frozen off. And my heart was a pile of ash. I felt like the statue in my dream, cracked from head to toe. One blow and I would shatter.

A huge shadow sailed over me, landing on the bed. The white wolf used its bulk to shift the pelts over me, then lay down. Its fur was chilled from the air, but I sank my hands in it anyway.

"I never asked for this," I warbled. I sounded pitiful, crying like a child. But I was lost. I felt small and fragile as a leaf, fallen from the tree into a great river, instantly swept away. I was drowning and my feet would never again touch the ground.

The wolf turned its great head toward me. After a while, it licked my face clean of tears with its broad, pink tongue.

"What am I going to do?" I clung to the wolf's neck, burying my face into its thick pelt.

∼

It was a long time before Jarl returned. By then Fenrir had cut down the deer and butchered it, lashed a few tree trunks together to lean against the entrance as a makeshift door, and built up a fire. I'd slept in the bed again, waking with a start when Jarl stomped in.

Jarl threw down a brace of dead pheasants, glowering at everything and nothing. I shrank into the bedding.

Jarl stopped before me, tossing a few long strips of leather onto the bed.

"Run again and I will hobble you," he said, looking pointedly at the leather ties. I glared down at them. What more could I do?

Fenrir set about plucking and spitting the pheasants to roast over the fire. Jarl stomped to the wood pile and started savagely thrusting logs into the fire.

Fenrir glanced at me, his mouth twisting in sympathy. "He is angry because you allowed yourself to suffer so long."

"What would I have done?"

"You could've come to us," Jarl said, slamming the last log down in a shower of sparks. "You belong with us."

I wrapped my arms around myself. "I belong to god."

Jarl stood and stretched out his arms. "Then why hasn't he saved you?"

Before I knew it, I'd flown off the bed and risen on tiptoe to scream in his face. "If you're so strong, why didn't you throw me down and take me when we first met? On the lawn of the abbey, in the light of the torches."

Gold shone in his eyes. "Is that what you wanted?"

"No!"

"Isn't it?" he crowded me backwards to the bed. "Why do you defy us? Why do you defy your nature?"

"Because it is not my nature. Or if it is, it is sinful and unholy."

"Who told you this?" Fenrir asked. He crouched by the fire, adjusting the cooking spit.

"The priest."

"Priests," Jarl scoffed. "Weak men who make rules others must follow."

"They are not weak—" I protested.

"They are. They made these rules to bind you." He snatched up the leather strips of the bed into his clenched fist, and shook it under my nose. "We are Berserkers. We are bound by nothing, least of all words chanted by puny priests."

I clenched my fists to keep from hitting him. "I am still bound."

"Yes, you are, little nun. And we will not let you leave. Push me, and I'll tie you to the frame." He threw the bonds on the bed and turned away, muttering. "I should punish you for running."

"Do it then," I spat.

I never saw him move. I ended up on my stomach, face pressed into the soft furs. Jarl's hard hand clamped on the back of my neck while the other jerked up my shift. I bellowed into the bed, clawing the pelts, writhing like an eel. His palm cracked down on my bare skin and I screamed. I kicked, but he smacked me again.

He knelt on the bed, capturing my flailing arms easily behind my back. "Is this what you wanted?"

I yelled and got a mouthful of fur. His palm caught the bottom of my buttocks and beat a tattoo on either cheek, painting them with pain. After a while, I stopped fighting and gripped the furs, surrendered to my punishment.

Jarl stopped to fondle my heated backside, and I held my breath, my heart pounding against the bed.

"I should've done this moons ago," he murmured, sounding calmer. His fingers dipped lower, straying close to a place no one had ever touched. Pleasure prickled in my belly, the feeling intense in contrast to my stinging bottom. There was the slightest touch to my tender folds, and then I wrenched away, flinging myself across the bed.

Jarl let me go. I rolled and drew the furs up to my neck. I expected to see him smirking, but instead he stood staring at the two fingers he'd used to touch me. "You're wet."

"No." My bottom throbbed and my core pulsed in reply. I grabbed a huge bear rug and dragged it over me. I was covered head to toe, but it was meager protection if the warrior decided to pounce.

But Jarl stayed where he was. He bent his head and sniffed his fingers before closing his mouth over them and sucking hard. He held my gaze the whole time. "Do not worry, Juliet. We will not give you pleasure. Not until you beg."

"I will never beg."

"Be careful, Juliet." His growl sounded like a threat. "You should not be so quick to vow what you do not—"

"Enough." Fenrir's deep voice echoed through the lodge. He rose from his crouch by the fire spit, dusting off his hands. "The meat is done. It's time to eat."

"Fine." Jarl stomped to the fire.

I burrowed into the pelts, wondering how long I could hide.

"Juliet?" Fenrir called. He was at the foot of the bed with a plate of half a pheasant.

My stomach growled.

"Come out," Jarl waved. "I call truce."

"Truce," I agreed, and slid out, wincing at the soreness in my bottom. I sat on the edge of the big bed and let my legs dangle as I picked the hot meat off the bones. The men sat on stumps around the fire.

For a while it was peaceful. Nothing but the crackling fire and snow falling beyond the makeshift door.

"You like pheasant?" Fenrir asked.

"I like food." I lifted a wing and tore the meat off it. I

sucked the bones clean of grease and cleaned my fingers. When I raised my head, I realized both warriors had stopped eating to watch me. They sat so still, they reminded me of wolves on the hunt.

I set the plate aside, flushing. "This is good, thank you. We did not eat much meat in the abbey."

"You did not have much in the abbey," Fenrir did not ask a question.

"No. I was an orphan. And then I took a vow of poverty."

Jarl leaned forward and spat bones into the fire. "Why?"

I glared at him. "I wished to serve God."

Jarl shook his head, muttering to himself.

"We don't understand," Fenrir said softly.

"Of course you don't," I burst out. "You don't even try."

"Tell us, then. Tell us of your god."

My mouth dropped open a moment before I found my voice. "You wish to know of my God?"

Jarl shrugged. "We have many. There is room for one more." He stretched out his legs.

I licked my lips. "There is but one god."

"Oh?" Jarl went to the cask in the corner and poured a horn of mead. He didn't seem overly interested but when I hesitated, he nodded for me to go on.

"He made all the world, and everything in it." I shifted in my seat. My bottom still prickled from my punishment.

"And how did he make it?"

"He spoke words." My own words came out quavery and unsure. "He spoke the world into being. He said "Light" and there was light."

"Words? He sounds like a priest." Jarl put the horn to his lips and drained it.

I twisted my hands together. "You are mocking me."

"Never," Fenrir said. He stroked his dark beard. "You gave yourself to this god, yes? Pledged your fealty?"

"I made vows. Holy vows." Could it be possible? Would they really listen to me? Perhaps I could convince them of my intent to hold myself apart from the world. To remain pure.

Perhaps I could convince them to let me go.

"You are a priestess," Fenrir said. "Did you lead the holy ceremonies?"

"No. The abbess did, at times. My role was to serve. To work and pray and live a worthy life."

"Why?" Jarl asked.

"Why?" I repeated, not understanding.

"Why would you do this?" Jarl leaned close. "What is the reward?"

Reward? "Service is its own reward."

Jarl scoffed.

"A warrior knows if he shows valor and dies in battle, he will go to Valhalla."

"What is Valhalla?" I shook my head when Jarl offered me his horn.

"A marvelous place. There's a great lodge and vast table. The warriors gather and war against each other until sundown. At night there's a great feast with endless mead. Then the next day, they do it all again." Jarl lifted his horn in a toast. "To Valhalla."

"Valhalla," Fenrir echoed, and both drained their horns. "Valhalla and Valkyries."

"Valkyries," Jarl slapped his knee.

"What are Valkyries?" I asked.

"Warrior women. Odin's daughters. Beautiful and deadly." Jarl winked at me. "They serve the worthy."

I rolled my eyes. Of course these warriors would believe

in an afterlife with endless fighting and feasting, with goddess-like beauties serving them. "That sounds like something a warrior would want to believe."

"It is," Jarl said.

"And you, Juliet?" Fenrir asked, leaning forward. "What is it you want to believe?"

My hand flew to my neck. "What?"

Jarl waved a hand. "Forget him. Where do you go when you die?"

"To heaven, if I am good. But that is not why I wish to be good and free of sin. I truly want to be pure and holy. To live a worthy life dedicated to God. Like the Virgin Mother."

"Virgin Mother," Jarl repeated, his face blank.

"Yes. She was pure and good of heart and chosen by God to be the vessel for his only begotten son."

Jarl squinted at the rafters. "So this Virgin bore your God a son."

"Yes," I nodded. "The Virgin Mother."

"Virgin Mother," Fenrir repeated slowly. "So she was untouched by a man, but a mother."

"Yes," I said, wishing I had paid better attention to the friar when he preached. Fenrir approached with a horn of mead and I was so flustered, I took it.

Jarl waited for me to take a sip before he said, "So she was like you."

I was so startled I almost dropped the horn. "What?"

"Little mother," Fenrir said. "You are a mother to all the children who know you."

"And yet you are untouched by any man." Jarl smirked at me.

"Is that why you cling to your vows? Do you hope to be a virgin mother, like your goddess?" Fenrir asked.

"No. I am nothing like her. I am a sinner, poor and

lowly." Why had I thought I could explain? The abbess would whip me if she heard my feeble attempts at theology. She'd spit with rage, *It is not for the likes of you to understand.*

"Then why, Juliet?" Jarl wasn't smirking anymore. He leaned forward, intently focused on me. "Why did you make the vow?"

"I don't know," I whispered.

The two warrior's brows furrowed in unison. I wasn't making sense. I was losing them.

"I mean, I-I wanted to," I stammered. "I wanted to be good. I wanted to be safe."

"Safe," Fenrir echoed and nodded. "That is why you cling to your beliefs."

I dropped the horn and it clattered to the ground. I pressed my hands to my ears. "*Kyrie eleison. Christos eleison.*"

"Juliet. Juliet." Gentle hands came to mine. They tugged lightly and I resisted but in the end my hands were captured in ones much larger than mine. I gazed into Fenrir's golden eyes. "Stop. Hush now. We are not angry with you. We seek only to understand."

I licked my lips. I was so hot, and my mouth was dry. My mouth still moved, forming shapeless prayers.

"How can she make us understand? She doesn't understand herself," Jarl muttered.

Fenrir growled in his direction. Jarl shot out of his seat and started pacing.

"I didn't mean that, Juliet," he said, running his hand through his hair so it stood up. "I meant only the things you were taught have no meaning, other than what you give them."

I was too shocked not to answer. "Are you saying there are no gods?"

Fenrir sighed deeply. Jarl rubbed the back of his neck.

"No," Jarl said. "That is, I do not deny the gods. But they never have granted me favor. Why should I give them more than their due?"

Fenrir pulled me into his arms, and I was too shocked to stop him. "Ignore him," he advised. "He is angry because the gods never answered his prayers."

"I never prayed to them," Jarl snapped.

"Your mother's prayers, then," Fenrir corrected patiently, and this time Jarl growled.

"Do not speak of my mother. I have never spoken of her to you." Jarl's eyes flared bright. Tension hung in the air between both warriors. I shifted uneasily on Fenrir's lap and his arms locked around me.

"You didn't have to." Fenrir's voice was still mild as he spoke to his warrior brother. He shifted me in his lap to explain, "We share memories."

"Is that the magic?" I asked, too overcome with curiosity to stop myself.

"It's the curse," Jarl said. He smacked the doorframe and walked out of the lodge. The tension leaked out of me, but the lodge felt strangely empty with him gone.

"We can speak mind to mind," Fenrir said. "And share thoughts, dreams. Sometimes memories, though not always intentionally. The connection comes unbidden. And then, yes, it does seem like a curse." He eased me into a new position on his lap, facing him. "Why did you take the vows, Juliet?"

"I thought it was what I wanted. I was an orphan, with no family. My mother's family gave me to the nuns when I was a few years old. I knew nothing but the abbey."

Fenrir listened patiently. He looked at me with such calm and a hint of something else—tenderness?—I could not meet his eyes.

I dropped my gaze to my lap. "When I came of age, I begged to stay. I promised to work hard and help take care of the orphans. I love the girls like sisters, for they were the only family I'd ever known. The abbess wanted to cast me out, but the friar took pity on me and said yes."

"What would they have done if you hadn't taken vows?"

I shivered. "I don't know. There were girls older than me. They came of age and disappeared. The friar said he'd found husbands for them."

"But you did not believe it."

"No, I—" I fell silent. "I felt something was wrong. But it was not my place to speak. In matters of the church, women are not to speak."

Fenrir sat back. "You were right to take vows."

I blinked. That was the last thing I expected him to say. "I was?"

His fingers combed through my hair. Soothing me. I leaned into his palm. "Those girls were not given to husbands, but to the Corpse King, to feed his growing power."

I sucked in a breath. He stroked my head, but I'd gone stiff and cold. "Truly?"

"Yes. Your vows saved your life. They kept you safe until we found you." His fingers sifted through my hair, then gave a little tug. "But now it's time to put them aside."

"Put them aside?" I shook my head, dizzy.

"Yes," Jarl said, stomping back inside. "Your vows saved you. But now we are here to protect you. And you must admit your god brought you to us."

I wrinkled my nose, ready to argue, but Fenrir tugged my hair so I turned back to him. "You say your god made the world and everything in it. Including you."

"*He knit me together in my mother's womb,*" I quoted. "Yes."

"Then he made you like this." His left hand settled on my chest and slid down over my breasts, leaving heat in its wake. "You were created thus, and filled with desire."

"No," I whispered.

"Yes," Fenrir insisted. "All these nights you've prayed for release. And your god allowed us to take you."

Oh, God, no. I closed my eyes.

"Your body burns in our presence. You were made for us, Juliet. As we were made for you." His hand covered my breasts, rubbing gently. A tide of golden pleasure rose, ready to sweep me away.

"No, no." I grabbed his arm. "This desire is a thorn in my flesh. I wish that I could cut it out."

"Juliet," Fenrir said, but I wouldn't hear another word. I kicked, trying to free myself.

"I have sinned. I have fallen short. I am damned. I must be cleansed and made new." I was babbling now. I clawed at Fenrir's hand, and when it fell away, I clawed at my own flesh.

"Stop," Fenrir ordered.

"Juliet." Jarl lifted me. His hand collared my throat, and he held my back to his front so he could murmur in my ear. "You have done wrong?"

"Yes, yes."

"Then you must be punished."

Relief flooded me and I went limp against him. "Yes."

"What if we were to punish you instead?"

"What?"

"We captured you. We have a right to you, according to our law."

I tried to shake my head, but Jarl held me fast. My pulse pounded against his hand. "What law is that?"

"The law of might." Jarl maneuvered me through the

lodge, towards the drying frame. His hand was still at my neck and his arm was around my waist. "You cannot stop us."

They were right. I could not. If God had meant for me to fight, he would've made me stronger.

"That's settled then. You are ours to punish and control." He positioned me between the posts of the frame and stretched my arms over my head to bind my wrists with the dangling strips of leather. My feet rested on an elevated platform that put my head closer to the bottom of their chin.

Fenrir approached, the firelight shining on his bare chest. "We will punish you. And then we will make you whole."

6

Juliet

Jarl stepped back, leaving my arms bound above my head. "You have no choice, Juliet," he reminded me. Then he took hold of my shift and ripped it from top to bottom.

I hung from the ties, my chest heaving as he stripped me naked. When he stepped back to view his handiwork, I pressed my pale legs together, trying to hide the dark thatch of hair at their apex.

But Fenrir knelt and tied my ankles apart until I stood on the platform, spread eagled. I could not escape. Jarl appeared in front of me and I jerked back as far as I could in my tethers.

"Easy," Fenrir steadied me with hands at my hips. His rough hands smoothed over me.

"Here." Jarl draped a cloth over my eyes. I tried to shake free, but he tied it behind my head.

"What—" I tried to ask, and one of them stuffed a piece of cloth in my mouth.

"The time for arguments is over," Jarl mocked. I cursed him. It came out muffled, but he understood all the same and laughed. "What happened to being silent before men?"

I screamed curses at him loud enough to hurt my throat. Then a mouth brushed the top of my thigh and my shout died to a whimper.

"Easy, Juliet," Fenrir said. His beard scraped my skin, so close to where my core throbbed. "Submit." And his thumbs spread my inner lips. Hot breath hit my center. I strained to close my legs.

"No," Jarl cracked his palm against my ass. "This is part of the punishment." He squeezed my bottom cheeks roughly, and spanked me again.

Fenrir's head brushed my belly. I curled away as much as I could as he swiped his tongue over my heated folds. He tickled and licked, scratching his jaw over my tender flesh and soothing the places his beard prickled.

There was a golden wave of heat brewing in my belly. My legs ached from trying to close. Jarl spanked me for that, smacking each cheek until my rear burned. But the pain was not as disturbing as the pleasant sensation curling out from my core. Nothing wrecked me like Fenrir's gentle tongue.

Desire sang through me, turning into delicate golden wisps that swooped and swirled and touched every part of me. I trembled, straining, no longer trying to escape but seeking Fenrir's mouth. And when he covered the whole of my sex with his hot mouth and thrust his tongue into my entrance, I cried out, contracting in anticipation of pleasure.

But before I could tip over the edge, he withdrew. I sobbed as my pleasure died.

"Shhhh," Fenrir petted me, stroking my upper thighs and planting a kiss on my cunny. "Not until you beg."

I shouted behind the gag, but it came out garbled. I wasn't even sure what I said.

"Not tonight." And Fenrir moved away.

Jarl gripped my chin. "Now we will mark you." He brushed a kiss to my forehead, then stepped back.

I tensed, waiting for the pain to come. I'd been beaten before.

Instead, someone kissed me again, this time on my jaw. Maybe it was Jarl, maybe Fenrir. The kisses were soft, but the beard chafing my skin felt like Jarl's. I shifted on my feet, dancing as the unseen warrior let his lips trail down my neck. His mouth licked and sucked, painting a line from my chin to my chest. He rubbed his beard over my breasts. I arched my back, welcoming the prickling sensation.

Someone else stroked my back. Fingers ran up and down, thrumming my skin until my body sang. These warriors played me like a lyre.

"This is not punishment," I breathed into my gag. Someone pulled it away and pressed a water skin to my lips. I drank in great gulps. A little water ran from my mouth and whoever offered me the water licked it up.

"What was that, little nun?" asked Fenrir from behind me.

I stiffened. I didn't need a reminder of what I was.

"This is not punishment," I said again.

"We have only just begun," Fenrir murmured and put his mouth to my shoulder. He bit lightly, then sucked hard enough to leave a red mark. He pressed his full body to mine. Sleek muscle and coarse hair. He was naked. I tried to shift away and his hardness poked my behind. His fangs nicked my skin and he kissed his way down my back. I arched backward as his beard tickled me. Lightning shot down my spine.

"Juliet," Jarl growled and fisted his hand in my hair. He drew my head back, pressing his bare chest to my front. A shudder went through him and shook me. His cock prodded my belly. I whimpered. He brushed his lips over mine and I angled my head, trying to kiss him back. "You are so sweet," he breathed. He tugged down the gag, grasped my chin. His mouth came down on mine and his tongue plunged inside. Desire surged between my legs and I rose to tiptoes.

Fenrir's mouth browsed over my buttocks, kissing and sucking the places Jarl had spanked before. A nip of his teeth struck sparks and fire roared through me. I hung between them, suspended in a dark world of pure sensation.

Then they drew away. I danced on my tether, turning this way and that, trying to find them.

A hand steadied my hip and Fenrir shushed me. He dragged something over my hair, steadying me when it caught in a snarl.

"It's a brush," he told me. "You have beautiful hair."

"So do you." I relaxed and let him brush out my hair. The long strokes soothed me until I floated. He reached around me and brushed the tops of my legs and I barely roused. The stiff bristles chafed but did not break the skin. He brushed my belly and breasts, and warmth rose and spread over the surface of my skin.

He rubbed the bristles over my freshly spanked buttocks and I hissed. My skin was tender.

"Is it punishment or is it a gift?" Fenrir murmured. "Pain is so close to pleasure." He rubbed the back of the brush over my heated bottom, then slapped my behind with the hard surface. I cried out.

"Enough?"

I shook my head and gripped the leather bindings, bracing myself. "More."

But instead of more pain, he took something soft and silky and rubbed it against my abused flesh. Fur. It tickled. He swirled the scrap of fur over my breasts and belly, and it felt like heaven on my abraded skin.

The soft fur went away and something else touched my skin. Five hard points, brushing over my belly. Something loomed close to me, big and growling low. The hair raised along my neck and when I turned my head, I caught a whiff of magic. Hot breath puffed over my cheek.

I was in the presence of the beast.

I stiffened and closed my eyes tight under the blindfold. My heart pounded faster.

The creature in front of me caught my hips. Its claws pricked me and I shrank away. It growled and I would've crumpled to the ground if I hadn't been tied.

Human hands caught me from behind and I stifled a shriek. "Enough," Fenrir said. I felt the beast retreat and I could breathe again.

The scrap of fur returned, rubbing me down and soothing me.

"You're doing well, Juliet." He dipped closer to the throbbing place between my legs but did not trespass there.

His lips came to my ear. "If you beg, I will make you feel good."

I shook my head. "No, please."

"Juliet..."

"Please," I whispered. "I need it to hurt."

He retreated and for a moment I was disappointed. But he wasn't gone long.

A whistle of air and something long and thin struck the front of my thighs. A switch. It whipped up and down my legs as I danced on tiptoe.

When it stopped

"More?" Fenrir asked.

I bit my lip and nodded. The switch struck my backside. He painted thin lines of pain up to my shoulder blades and down my back, bottom, and calves. One of them even tugged my bounds until I hung higher, my feet barely touching the ground, so the other could whip the bottoms of my feet.

When they eased off my bounds, I remained on tiptoe, sniffling. My body was covered with little welts.

"My turn," Jarl growled. He spun me around and hooked a hard arm around my middle, lifting me. My relief didn't last because he rubbed my bottom with a smooth wooden surface. Whatever he held was much bigger than the hairbrush. I tensed.

He paddled me softly at first, then hard enough the crack echoed in the lodge. Every so often he paused to soothe me, rubbing my aching rear with the paddle. Then he'd begin again.

Tears dripped down my face by the time Fenrir took his place.

"Almost done," Fenrir crooned. I leaned into him. I hurt all over. A good hurt. Inside my chest, I felt clean.

"Lean back, Juliet," he ordered. I did and he tipped me back further. My bare breasts were offered up to him.

A prickly leaf brushed my skin. I jumped and cried out, but Fenrir held me fast as he rubbed nettles over my breasts. I choked on the sting.

"It's over." Someone cut the bounds holding my arms above my head and Fenrir caught me and carried me to the bed where he lay me down on the soft pelts. I whimpered as my back hit the fur.

"Shhhh, you did well." He stroked the hair back from my face.

I throbbed in every corner of my body. My breasts prickled from their brush with the tiny barbs on the nettle leaves. My back and legs were striped from the switches and my buttocks were hot and sore. And yet all the aches grew faint and weak when compared with the throbbing between my legs. It was as if the pain and need flowed together into one growing wave of sensation, threatening to crash through me.

I reached for the blindfold and someone stayed my hand. "Not yet," Jarl growled. He pinned my wrists to the bed.

My sigh shuddered through me.

"We punished you. You are absolved." Fenrir gentled me with a hand on my breastbone. "Now, we will make you feel good."

A horn of mead came to my lips and I drank deeply.

Someone else was soothing something over my breasts. A balm of some sort, thick and sticky.

A finger touched my lips. My tongue flicked out and the sweetness burst on my tongue. I smacked my lips.

"Honey," I said.

"Yes," Fenrir said, and licked between my breasts. He brushed honey over my nipple and closed his mouth over it. All the sting went away as he prodded my nipple with his tongue. Pleasure flashed from my breast to my cunny. I arched off the bed, my ears filling with my moans.

I felt Fenrir move away and Jarl took his place. He

smeared a whole handful of honey over my abraded chest and leaned down to lap it up. His beard pricked my skin and became soaked in honey, so much that when he lifted his head to kiss me, the rich taste filled my mouth. I sucked on his lip, savoring the sweetness.

Fenrir worked his way down, stroking honey over my belly, the tops of my legs. Jarl licked up my neck, his beard tickling, making me shiver. Fenrir lapped long strokes up my thighs, growing closer and closer to my aching cunny.

When he nuzzled the valley between my legs, I squirmed. He swirled two fingers over the tops of my thighs and dipped between them, painting honey into my sex.

"Oh no." I twisted, trying to escape, but two sets of firm hands grabbed my legs.

And then, oh, then they licked me. Two rough tongues danced and delved—into my belly button, into the crevice between my legs, pressing further and further. They were everywhere. A rough hand covered my breast, squeezing. Another gripped my knee and drew it out and up, holding me open. My body held no secrets then. A mouth covered my cunny, licking deep between my folds. I pushed my sore bottom into the bed but I could not get away.

And then he moved away and someone—Jarl—covered my sex with honey again so he could take his turn licking me. His beard scraped up my inner thighs and then his whole face pressed between my legs.

"No, no," I cried out and two fingers pushed into my mouth, rubbing honey onto my tongue. By the time they withdrew, only to be replaced by Fenrir's mouth, I was overcome. Fenrir murmured against my lips and gave me kiss after drugging kiss. I dug my fingers into his hair, gripping him close. He started to kiss down my chin again and I dragged him back. But he caught my wrists and rose over me.

The warriors rolled me over. They tied my hair back and spread the honey over my back, paying attention to each welt. Then the backs of my legs where the switch had bit my skin.

And at last they kissed my buttocks, scraping my chastised flesh with their rough beards, then soothing it with their tongues. I squirmed and they held me down. Firm hands gripped and parted my cheeks—they drizzled honey and licked there too. I was panting and pressing myself into the furs, my back arched to offer my aching center to their mouths even as I tried to wriggle away.

The bed creaked as they rose up over me. Fingers stroked wet folds and I thrashed harder.

"Please, please," I said.

Jarl chuckled. "When I said you would beg, I didn't know it would be so soon."

"Please," I was shaking when they flipped me over. Fenrir knelt between my legs, body gleaming in the firelight. Without thinking, I reached for him.

He pinned my wrists and stretched out over me, his weight settling on my needy cunny, just enough to ease the ache. His hair curtained my head as he stopped my mouth with his. I couldn't move far, but everything in me strained upwards.

"All right, Juliet. We will give you what you need." And again he kissed down my body, taking care to swirl his tongue over my sore spots and soothe them. My body shimmered with sensation.

Fenrir lay his head against my thigh, watching me as he pushed a finger inside my body. My toes curled so hard they cramped.

"Easy." Fenrir stroked lightly inside me. "You don't have to fight for it. Just breathe and take what I give you." He withdrew his fingers and rose up again so he could grind the heel of his hand against my sopping center. Little sparks of sensation flew up, igniting a firestorm. My spine bowed as pleasure coiled tight, past the breaking point. My legs started to shake uncontrollably.

Fenrir was still watching me closely. "That's it. Surrender."

My own cries filled my ears and pleasure washed outwards. All the pain I'd felt was swallowed up in the maelstrom. I was tossed and tumbled, helpless in the storm of sensation. My climax shook me in its grip.

Fenrir pressed down on my sex, grounding me.

"My turn," Jarl growled. I barely sensed Fenrir shifting out of the way before I felt Jarl stretched over me. He pinned my wrists the same way Fenrir had. Dropping his knee, he pressed it against my still pulsing center. He rocked slowly over me. I blinked as sparks rose behind my eyes. And as my climax broke over me again, Jarl set his teeth against my neck and scraped them over my pulse, pushing me ever higher.

7

Juliet

I BARELY REMEMBERED the rest of the night. The warriors worked over me, wrung me out with as much pleasure as they'd given me pain. Climax after climax crashed over me. I came so many times, I teetered on the edge of pain again, and begged them to stop.

"One more," Fenrir insisted. Jarl held me down and I screamed myself hoarse and Fenrir pulled another round of pleasure from my cunny with his lips and tongue. My orgasm swelled over me, a giant wave rising and rising until it was too large to hold back. It broke over me and I lost my grip on myself. I felt nothing, saw nothing, knew nothing but oblivion.

I barely roused when they washed me clean with a cloth dipped in heated water. I caught only a few glimpses of my reddened skin before my eyelids were too heavy to prop open. Fenrir rolled my limp body in a fur. The warriors lay down on either side of me and took turns stroking my hair and I surrendered to sleep.

~

I woke to weak light across my face. The sun was high enough to delve through the cracks in the makeshift door. I'd slept through the night and into the day beyond.

Jarl and Fenrir slumbered next to me. I was still curled between them, though the fur had slipped down. We were all naked, but I did not fret. I now wanted to share my nakedness with these men.

Slowly I rose and slipped out of bed, throwing a fur around my shoulders to keep off the chill. The fire had been built up and fresh wood stacked beside it, the warriors taking care to keep the lodge warm. They'd let me sleep.

Barefoot, I hastened to drink a little water and relieve myself. At first my limbs were wobbly and felt wrung out, but after a moment I found new strength. My legs and breasts bore disappointingly few marks. Even my buttocks were barely bruised. My cunny had borne the most punishment. It was pink and puffy, but even as I inspected it, it throbbed in anticipation for more.

The biggest difference was on the inside. My chest was light, my head high. The weight I'd carried was gone. The pain had scoured my insides clean.

I washed my face and shook out my hair.

The cold bit at my backside until I wriggled back into bed. The warriors gave no sign that they'd woken. I'd never known them to slumber so deeply. Were they as affected by our night together as I had been?

In sleep, they seemed less intimidating. I rolled to face Fenrir. A few strands of his hair had caught in his beard and I brushed it back. Fenrir's long lashes fluttered but he remained still, a slumbering mountain.

Jarl let out an uneasy grumble and I shifted to face him. His brow was creased so I stroked it gently. The wrinkles smoothed under the pads of my fingertips.

Emboldened, I did what I'd always wanted to do. I traced the dark outline of his tattoos, following the lines with my finger. On the first pass his eyes slitted open, but he didn't stop me.

I examined the swirls down his forearm, then switched to his chest. A rumble under my palm made me snatch my hand back.

"Don't stop," Jarl said in a voice made guttural by sleep. So I didn't. I stroked the painted skin stretched over his collarbone, and traced the ridges between his muscles. The lower my hand got, the more rapidly his chest rose and fell. His hips shifted and I withdrew, returning to touch his face. He closed his eyes as I brushed my fingertips over his eyebrows. When he opened them, I blinked against the flash of gold.

"Juliet," he growled and shifted closer. The hair on the back of my neck prickled. I was seconds away from being pulled under him and ravaged.

I smiled and rubbed a finger over his bottom lip. He caught the tip of my finger in his teeth. The nip sent a jolt to my core.

I was close enough to feel his hot breath on my face. "Why did your mother name you 'Jarl'?"

He tugged my hand down between us. I felt the rough trail of coarse hair leading from the middle of his chest down, down. I flattened my palm over the hard muscles in his abdomen. He spread his hand over mine, trapping it. "She wanted me to become one."

"Become a jarl?"

"Yes." He laced his fingers over mine. Slowly, he started to drag both our hands lower.

He was telling me something important. I better find out what before our hands reached the intended destination.

I licked my lips and his eyes dropped to my mouth. "Why?"

"Because the Jarl was my father. But my mother was a slave."

I sucked in a breath and let Jarl coax our hands another inch lower. "What happened?"

"The Jarl didn't believe I was his son. Or he didn't care." He leaned forward suddenly, so his lips were at my ear. "But it didn't matter because I grew up strong. My mother protected me. She raised me well. Many times she sacrificed her own food to see I didn't starve. And I grew into a man, bigger and more powerful than my father would ever be."

My hand rested in the taut hollow above his hips. His skin was hot as if a fire burned in his chest. His breath came in gusts and his muscles were hard as stone. But he was still, as if frozen.

I drew my head back so I could look him in the eye. "Did you kill him?"

"No." Regret colored Jarl's growl. "My half brother, his true son did. But I fought for my rightful position, and gained it. For my mother and myself. You see, Juliet." His fingers closed around my wrist. "This world belongs to the ones who are strong enough to take it. That is how it is. That is how it always will be." And he pushed my hand down until his thick cock throbbed against my palm. Coarse hair scored my skin. I gulped, but Jarl did not force me further. He held still and waited.

"You think to take whant you want?" I raised a brow.

He nodded, but his eyes were wide. I raised my chin and moved the barest inch to kiss his lips. "No." I smiled at him and curled my fingers around his stiff length. "You cannot take what is given freely." I leaned back then, enough to see what I was doing and marvel at this huge warrior quivering in the palm of my hand. My own body quickened as I slid my fingers over him, exploring the veins winding around his shaft, the flared head and slit leaking fluid like drops of dew. I freed my other hand so I could better grip him. My fingers wouldn't reach the whole way around. My thumb played with the tip and came away wet. Without thinking, I raised my thumb to my mouth and sucked it clean.

Jarl's entire body jerked. "Juliet," he groaned and claimed my mouth. His kiss seared through me. I surged against him, pressing my aching breasts against his chest, writhing to stimulate them.

"Show me," I begged, breathless. "Show me what pleases you."

He rolled me to my back and rose up over me, his cock in hand. As I watched he slowly slid the sheath of his grip up and down until his cock jerked. I sat up and touched the weeping tip, fascinated. I cupped my right hand over his and let my arm move with his.

"Now you." He took his hand away and molded mine over his turgid rod. My hand looked small and pale in comparison. As I slid my fingers up and down, the monster swelled larger. I squeezed slightly and Jarl groaned. I dipped my head to lick the salty fluid leaking from the tip and Jarl sputtered curses.

"Did that hurt?" I asked.

"No," Jarl grunted, but his voice sounded pained.

A chuckle came from Fenrir. The warrior was awake and lying on his back, one arm propped behind his head, the other fisting his long cock. "Do it again, Juliet. It will kill him."

I started to loosen my grip and Jarl's hand covered mine. "Don't stop." He moved his hand and mine along with it until I was jacking him faster. His hips thrust raggedly, pushing his cock into my hand. "Ah, Juliet. Keep doing that. Just like that." The first spurt of seed onto the bed made me jump. Jarl pushed me down and squeezed my hand around his cock so tight it seemed he milked the cum out of himself, onto my bare belly. "Yes," he murmured, dropping his hand and smearing his essence over my skin, over my collarbone and between my breasts. He offered a finger to my lips until I opened my mouth and tasted him. Bitter salt coated my tongue.

"Come here, lovely." Fenrir lay back. I crawled to him and he maneuvered me back. "Lie between my legs." When I did, he lifted my hair away from my face. "Lick me now. Gently. No teeth." His cock lay long against his leg. I cupped it in my hand and worked my mouth over it, swirling my tongue over the heated tip. He fisted a hand in my hair, moving my head where he wanted it. I did my best to take his cock, salt and heat filling my mouth and bumping the back of my throat until I choked. Tears came to my eyes and he brushed them away, murmuring comforting things, only to force my head down further as my hands pressed into the bed. "Good girl, that's it."

He lay me back and straddled my chest. His big thighs pinned me down. The muscles strained as his cock bobbed in front of my lips. I took a deep breath and opened for him, letting his cock slide in and out of my mouth. He kept a grip in my hair, fisting tight enough to sting my scalp. I tried to breath and swallow him down as deep as I could.

I was panting when he drew back and fisted his cock in front of my face until he spilled his seed between my breasts. My chest rose and fell as Fenrir did what Jarl did and spread it over my skin. A baptism of sorts. I was soaked in their essence, coated in it.

"What do you want, Juliet?" Jarl knelt beside me. His cock still jutted out from the dark nest of hair between his legs. My own cunny throbbed at the sight.

"You," I whispered. "I want you." And I spread my legs wide.

Jarl shackled my ankle in his big hand. "You are sure you want this?" He tipped me over and smacked my rear cheeks. I squirmed as he and Fenrir knelt on either side of me. They took turns spanking me until the heat flooded my bottom and my sex, then flipped me back over. Fenrir's body covered me and I reached up to grip his shoulders. "I want you."

"If we take you, there's no going back." He rocked over me, rubbing his cock against my cunny. I wrapped my legs around his hips, drawing him closer, begging for more. "We will not let you go."

"Don't let me go," I said. "I'm yours."

8

Jarl

JULIET LAY HEAVING in the furs. Her small body glimmered with the pearly sheen from our seed. She bore our scent from head to toe. *As it should be,* the beast whispered, and I agreed.

Fenrir stretched over her, his cock rubbing against her entrance. Heat flushed our little nun's cheeks. Her dark curls stuck to her sweaty skin. Between her legs, her skin was dark pink and puffy from all the attention we'd given it. She never looked more beautiful.

She is small and will find it difficult to take us, Fenrir spoke to me mind to mind.

I will do it, brother, if you are afraid.

Fenrir gave me a look and I bared my teeth at him. Heat flooded my body and my skin prickled. Fur rippled down my back and up my arms—the beast, taking over. We needed to fuck our mate, and soon.

He sat back on his haunches and probed her entrance with his fingers. "So small and tight."

Juliet growled, her hips rising. "Do it," she said.

Fenrir shuddered. His own control was slipping. "It will hurt, little one." His voice was guttural, inhuman.

"I am strong." Juliet jerked her body down on his fingers.

In a fluid movement, Fenrir stretched over her again and reached down to open her to accept him. A tremor went through his big body as he entered her. A pause while both Juliet and Fenrir stared down at the thick rod slowly impaling her delicate folds. He retreated and she gripped him harder, her nails drawing blood.

His face taut with tension, Fenrir nudged at her entrance again.

"Give it to me," Juliet ordered.

"Patience, little one."

"No," she snarled. "I have waited—"

He snapped his hips forward, shoving his cock inside. She gasped, clawing at his shoulders.

"Wait," Fenrir ground out. "Stretch for me. Do you feel that? I'm inside you."

Juliet curled into him. Her teeth sought his shoulder and when she couldn't reach, she scraped her teeth along his chest muscle and bit down. He roared, surging into her. She cried out, her nails scoring his back.

"Almost there," he growled.

"A little pain, and it will never hurt again," he vowed. He sank his teeth into her left shoulder.

Juliet screamed and pain sizzled along the edges of my awareness. The ache washed my mind clear. The beast retreated, satisfied. My fangs throbbed in my mouth.

It is well, brother. You did right. Next it would be my turn. I would hold her small form in my arms and sink into her softness. I will claim her innocence. And I would mark her so no one would wonder who she belonged to.

***

Juliet

I BARELY FELT when Fenrir left and Jarl took his place above me. My body was open, unfolding like a flower, and it was nothing to widen my legs and accept Jarl into my body. He braced himself with tattooed arms on either side of my head. As he slid inside, he bent and sank his teeth into my right shoulder, giving me a bite to match Fenrir's on my opposite side.

It is done. The voice bloomed deep in my mind. A presence hovering on the edge of my thoughts. Jarl and Fenrir. And beyond them, a dark shape bigger than the sky, a blackness that obliterated everything it touched. The beast. I jerked away and found myself still in the bed on my back, caged by a huge warrior's body.

A growl rumbled deep in Jarl's chest. I clawed at his back, marking him in my own way. My vision filled with the dark whorls and shapes of his inked skin as he worked over me. His chest and abdomen flexed in mesmerizing rhythm. Where the tattoos left off a dark line of hair began, trailing down to the crisp dark nest around his cock. I reached down and touched the place where he joined me. He put his hand over mine and rubbed, finding the place that triggered a white hot burn. Lightning flashed down my legs. I cried out, crashing back into that dark place in my mind where the beast rose up and swallowed me whole. I was consumed, darkness closing over my head. But I felt nothing but pleasure. Climaxes wracked my body. I opened my mouth, but my screams were swallowed by the night.

Juliet? Fenrir's voice, and Jarl's.

I'm here. Somehow, I was still alive.

Come back to us.

I grasped their soothing whispers like a tether and let it drag me back to consciousness. Two worried faces hung over me.

"I saw it. The beast."

"It's never far. It won't hurt you."

"I know." Ever since I'd known them, I hadn't been afraid. I'd always known I was safe. I'd seen the worst of them, the beast, and knew it would do anything to protect me.

They took turns rutting over me. Again and again, deep into the night. Tingles spread under my skin, reviving my sore body. The magic that made them monsters, making me whole.

You are the best part of us, the warriors told me. We lay tangled together as the sun came up. As the light broke over the world, I fell asleep in my warriors' arms.

9

Juliet

I WOKE ALONE in the low light. Jarl and Fenrir must have gone to fetch firewood or hunt for food. I didn't know whether it was dusk or dawn, or whether I'd slept a day or a year. The ache between my legs told me what I had done.

I sat up and tried to comb out my hair, but it was too tangled. My shift was gone, torn away. I was naked, barefoot, cold. The bed was still warm from the warrior's bodies, but I could not return to it. The beauty of our night together was shattered.

What had I done? I'd broken my vows.

I staggered from the lodge. As soon as I stepped outside, my feet ached from the cold ground, but I welcomed the hurt as punishment for what I'd done. All the lovely glow that had filled me after my punishment was gone, leaving me barren and empty inside. The good was gone, only the ugly was left. Only I was left.

I sank down, my hands over my face. Everything inside me welled up and I sobbed.

Jarl found me there, crouched and crying in the mud. He cursed and dropped the firewood he'd chopped, and rushed to wrap me in his robe before carrying me inside. He bundled me on the bed and left my side to build the fire higher.

I curled onto my side and cried as he paced back and forth. A wave of magic, and I sensed the dark form of the beast, prowling back and forth like a wild animal at the mouth of a cave.

Fenrir returned soon after, melting from the shadows. His shape was normal. He felt the pull of the beast but did not succumb to it. He set a brace of rabbits on a stone by the fire, moving slowly as if not to startle either of us. *What happened?* he asked as Jarl prowled past him.

She is rejecting us. She believes she has sinned.

"Calm down, brother."

She cannot leave us! Jarl roared.

"She's not leaving," Fenrir said. He moved between me and the fire. After a while, his weight sank into the bed beside me. "Juliet, come."

I pushed him away, but he lifted me to his lap. He had food and drink and met my resistance with calm patience.

"Now," he said when I had eaten and drank my fill. "Tell me why you are distraught."

"I am not Juliet." I said in a hollow voice. "I am someone else."

"No." He kissed my shoulder. "You are still you."

"I am undone." I pushed back the mess of my hair, but it fell over my face. Fenrir moved behind me. With patient hands, he bundled my hair back and began to brush the strands.

"The abbess was right." My voice cracked with sorrow. "I am a wild and unholy creature."

"You were born wild, but you are not unholy." Fenrir bent and kissed my shoulder. "We have let loose the ties that bound you. Now you are free."

"How can you say that?" I rubbed my chest. I did not feel free. I felt a great weight on my chest, stones in my heart.

Why this guilt? Jarl spoke directly into my mind. *Your priest would make you someone you were not.*

"But I am wicked," I cried.

"So you say. But I see no wickedness in you. Where is your proof?" He caught my hand when I would scratch furrows into my chest and closed his own huge hand around it.

I sat in his lap, quivering like a rabbit in a trap. "I have lain with two men."

"We forced you, remember? You had no choice."

That was not entirely true, and we both knew it. But I couldn't say that. "It doesn't matter."

"Juliet," Fenrir sighed. "Look at Jarl."

The tattooed warrior was fully Changed into a beast. The giant monster filled the doorway. The top of its dark furred head almost touched the lintel. It's back tensed, arching, as if any moment it would point its snout at the sky and howl.

"Tell him to come back to you," Fenrir ordered.

I parted my lips and Fenrir pushed two fingers into my mouth, silencing me. *Not that way,* his deep voice echoed in my mind.

Jarl. I thought hard. There was a monster in my mind, a

dark and angry shape. Hurt, abandoned. My heart cracked. *Come back to me.*

As I watched, the beast straightened, the fur disappearing, leaving a clean jaw and Jarl's sharp nose. Jarl the man emerged from the monstrous form. The final swirls of black fur faded into the dark markings on his smooth-skinned chest. He stretched, naked, and smirked when he caught me staring.

"Do you see?" Fenrir murmured. "In your presence, the beast is calm."

Jarl picked up the makeshift door and set it against the opening, blocking out the night. He returned to the bed and stretched out beside me, picking up my hand and squeezing it. I grabbed his hand and held it between my own, studying it for any trace of claw or fur. But it was a normal hand.

"Tamed by your voice," Jarl said. He sounded almost smug, but I didn't understand why.

"You have made us whole," Fenrir said, and slid me off his lap so I lay between them. "You have this power. Why would you deny it?"

I shook my head. I was so tired. "The priest said—"

"The priest is dead," Jarl growled. He still sounded like the beast. "Thorbjorn killed him."

Fenrir gripped my arm. "The priest was punished for his sins against Sage, Thorbjorn's mate. The man was evil, Juliet. He was not chaste or pure. He broke the very laws he preached to you."

Was it true? I searched Fenrir and Jarl's faces. But I didn't have to search their minds. I had my own memories from my time in the abbey, first as an orphan, then as a nun. I lived by rules of poverty and chastity, bore their weight and had been broken by them. And yet the man who'd never missed a moment to shout at me of my sin was guilty of despicable acts.

My face crumpled. "Everything I've known is a lie."

"It was, little mate. But now you are free."

"No," I moaned over the pain in my chest. "I do not know how to live free."

Fenrir sat back. He was silent a long time, regarding my words. "Then we will bind you to us. One way or another."

∽

I DREAMED of a monster roaring through the forest. The dark shape rushes the magical boundary at the foot of the mountain. The bodies of the enemy rush him and fall, limbs snap like dry branches and the scent of rotting flesh rises in waves to choke him.

I jerked awake, clawing at the sunlight air. I knew without looking around the lodge that Jarl was gone. The fire was cold and at first, I feared both warriors had abandoned me. Then Fenrir came to my side.

"Come, Juliet. The sun is high."

"Where did Jarl go?" I clutched the fur. My body still trembled as if it expected the enemy to rush me at any moment.

"He went ahead to clear a way for us." Fenrir laid a new dress on the bed beside me. I touched it before I could stop myself, amazed by the fine woolen garment. It was a rich purple, a color too fine for a peasant. Way too fine for an orphan girl turned nun. Not that the Berserkers would care. They brought me a dress fit for a queen and I must wear it. They'd torn all my other clothing to shreds.

"What does it mean, Jarl is clearing the way for us?" I asked as I dressed.

"You'll see." Fenrir produced a pair of fur-lined boots

and knelt to put them on my feet. He tugged me up and ran his hands down my bodice. His fingers stroked over the wool and I felt them as if he plucked my bare skin. My body hummed under his touch, a tune only he could play.

Too soon he took his hands away. "Come. We are leaving today."

"Where are we going?" I wriggled my toes in my new boots.

"You'll see." He grinned and I blinked at the sight. I rarely saw him smile.

With Fenrir's help, I braided my hair into a thick braid. He shouldered a large pack and adjusted his belt, checking the long knife and axe strapped to his waist. Then he took my hand and led me out of the lodge to face the day. We turned down the mountain path, but instead of avoiding the boundary line, he marched me straight toward it. There was no sign of the Grey Men, the dead beings the Corpse King raised for his army. But my stomach still flipped the closer we got to leaving the witches' protective bubble.

"Is it safe?" I toed the line between the living meadow and the churned mud where many *draugr* had patrolled.

"It is now," Fenrir gripped my hand and gripped a long knife in the other. "But we must hurry." He tugged me over the boundary. I felt the magic roll over my face, like I'd pushed through a curtain of water. We broke onto the other side, panting.

"Run," Fenrir was still grinning as if it were all a game. Was he mad? We raced for the trees. My feet pounded the ground and my new boots served me well.

We reached the tree line but kept running. He didn't let us slow until we were deep in a grove of pine. "Where are the *draugr*?" I asked.

"Jarl drew them off."

Jarl? I startled. As soon as his name bloomed in my mind, he answered.

I'm here. He answered in the voice of the beast, and thrust an image into my mind. I Saw his monstrous arms and paws. He stood in a clearing, leaning on a double-headed axe. At his feet were piles of bones. The Grey Men, destroyed.

There will be more. I scent another great force, marching to surround the mountain. But I have cleared your route.

"Come, Juliet." Fenrir shrugged off his pack. He crouched and bid me climb on his back. "Put your arms around my neck. We have leagues to go, and we must be back by dusk."

I hung on, wrapping my legs around his waist. He hitched me closer and took off. The forest blurred.

We journeyed this way, at Berserker speed, for several hours. Fenrir never paused and never seemed to tire.

"Will you tell me where we are going?" I asked when he let me down to drink at a stream and stretch my cramped legs.

"No. It will ruin the surprise." He lifted me again.

"At least tell me how much longer," I grumbled.

"Tell me a story," he said as he set off.

"A story? About what?" I closed my eyes to the trees passing with dizzying speed.

"Anything. You."

I bit my lip. I did not have any stories I wished to tell about me. But I had often told stories to the orphans. "Once there was a man named Jonah, who was a prophet. But he ran from God, and tried to escape by sailing across the sea..."

The sun was high in the sky when we came to a meadow full of flowers and he let me down for good. My voice was hoarse from talking. I'd told the story of Jonah and the whale, Noah and the ark, Balaam and the ass, and Gideon and his army. Fenrir enjoyed the stories with fighting best.

I arched my back and swung my arms, loosening my tight muscles. Fenrir had set me in a patch of bluebells. I bent to pick one, and when I straightened, a large, dark form stepped out of the shadows.

It was Jarl. The sunlight slid off his bare shoulders as he strode to me. He wore a pair of ragged breeches and held a shield and double-headed axe. But he was fully a man. I heaved a sigh as he set down his weapon and took up my hand.

"I dreamed you were a monster."

"I am a monster." He kissed my fingers. They were cold and he nuzzled them, warming them with his breath. "But more than that, I am yours."

"You missed the stories," I said, drawing my hand back.

"I did not. Fenrir shared them with me. Gideon's was the best." Jarl winked at me and stepped back as Fenrir approached.

"Well fought," Fenrir greeted his brother and tossed Jarl a pair of boots and a leather jerkin. Jarl dressed quickly. The jerkin was new, as were the boots, but the well-dressed man who wore them was barely more civilized than the half-naked warrior who'd strode from the woods. Especially when he strapped the shield and axe to his back.

"Do you enjoy fighting?" I asked.

"Yes." Jarl took my hand again.

"Is that why you became a Berserker?"

"Yes," he said more soberly. "But that was not the same."

I cocked my head to the side. "How do you mean?"

"Now we have someone worth fighting for." He tugged me into him and gripped the base of my braid. He kissed me, his beard scraping my face. He plunged his tongue into my mouth, plundering. I was gasping when he let me come up for air.

Fenrir cleared his throat loudly. "Not here, brother. Not yet."

I furrowed my brow, wondering what he meant. Jarl laughed and released me. "A little further, Juliet."

Fenrir also wore the jerkin and boots and breeches he'd worn before, but now they were brushed clean of mud. He'd tied his long hair back. With a grin, he smoothed his thumb over the chafed patches around my mouth. He picked up the bluebells that had fallen out of my hand and tucked a spray behind my ear.

"What is going on?" I asked. Both warriors wore grins, but pressed their lips together at my question. They were hiding something.

"You'll see," Fenrir beckoned me to follow. He took my right hand and Jarl took the other.

"It's a surprise."

"Will I like this surprise?"

"Yes. At least, we hope you will."

I sighed and let them pull me along. By the time we'd emerged from the woodland meadow, their excitement gripped me and I happily trotted between them. We came to a clearing that held a small stone hut. My steps slowed, but Fenrir and Jarl guided me straight to it.

"Hello? Who's there?" A man scurried out, wearing monk's robes. His tonsured pate gleamed in the light.

"Father, we are here to say our vows," Fenrir said in his deep voice. He took my arm and tugged me next to him. My mouth was hanging open. So was the friar's. His wide eyes took in the huge warriors—their rough garb, their shining weapons.

"To be joined in holy matrimony?"

"Yes," Jarl said, cocking an eyebrow at the tiny chapel. "I wish to be married in the tradition of your god."

The friar opened and closed his mouth once or twice, gaping like a fish. "Of course, of course. And you are baptized in the Holy Church?"

"Yes," Jarl lied.

I must have made a sound because Fenrir's hand tightened on mine.

"If the answer was no," Fenrir asked, "would you still do the rites?"

"Well, ah," the priest stammered. "I am only sanctioned to join two baptized in the eyes of God."

"She serves your god," Fenrir pointed to me.

"I am baptized," I said.

"Ah well, then." The priest cleared his throat. "You should not be unequally yoked. So says the Apostle Paul."

"Huh," Jarl snorted. "No one's getting yoked."

My cheeks burned twin flames.

"Perhaps, Father, you might make an exception," I said quietly.

"Perhaps, perhaps," the friar agreed, taking out a cloth and mopping his face and bald head.

Fenrir stepped forward. The friar cringed when the giant warrior held up his fist but soon realized what Fenrir held: a leather bag bulging with coin. Silently, Fenrir turned it over and let the coins spill out. They clinked to the ground, a small pile of gold. The friar blinked at it.

"Perhaps it will be all right," the man bobbed his tonsured head. "Would you like to come inside?"

Jarl grimaced and ducked his head inside the the chapel door to peer at the dark, dank space.

"No," he said, and I hid a smile. His shoulders would

barely fit through the door. There was no way both Jarl and Fenrir would fit.

My smile fell away. Which warrior was I marrying? Did it matter?

"Very well," the priest said, his eye on the gold. "One moment. Wait right here." He disappeared into the tiny church and returned with a heavy gold cross, a cup of wine and a small plate that contained the Host. These he set on the stone wall. "You wish to begin immediately?"

"Yes," Jarl said. His voice held a tinge of growl.

"Yes, thank you, Father," I said, and grabbed Jarl's hand. *Please don't turn into the beast.*

Jarl looked down at me, a golden glint in his eye. Fenrir had retreated behind us. By unspoken agreement, it was settled. I was to marry Jarl.

"Very good." The priest was practically rubbing his hands together in excitement. "First, you must confess your sins and be absolved." He turned to Jarl and motioned for the warrior to go with him a few steps away for privacy.

Jarl did not budge. "What sins?"

"All your sins." The priest scurried back to stand before us when he realized the warrior wasn't going to follow. "How long has it been since your last confession?"

"A long time," Jarl said slowly, stroking his beard.

"Decades," Fenrir muttered with a laugh and I frowned at him.

"It's all right," the priest encouraged. "You can sum them up."

Jarl was still rubbing his bearded chin. "What exactly count as sins?"

The priest's eyes bulged. "Well," he said after a pause. "The usual. There are many types of sin—"

"Can you give me a list?"

The priest took a deep breath. "Well, first there are grave sins. Adultery, fornication, uncleanness, lasciviousness, idolatry, witchcraft, hatred, variance, emulations, wrath, strife..." he trailed off as Jarl started nodding.

"Is that all?" Fenrir asked.

"Um, no. There's also heresies, envies, drunkenness—"

"I've definitely done that one," Jarl said.

"Revellings," the priest's voice faltered a little. "M-murders—"

"That too," Jarl said at the same time Fenrir asked, "What about war?"

"What about it?" The priest dabbed the cloth at his shiny brow.

"Well, we've killed many men. But was it murder?" Fenrir rubbed his chin. The friar looked like he would faint.

"Doesn't matter," Jarl shrugged. "I'm pretty sure I've murdered a few men outside of battle. Just for fun. Is that all of the sins?"

The friar licked his lips. "Well, no. Those are simply the gravest ones. There're also the vices. Pride, avarice, envy, wrath, lust—"

Jarl waved a hand. "I think it'll be faster to say I've done them all."

"We don't have much time," Fenrir added.

"All right. All right." The friar looked as if he wished he could dart back into the church and hide. He backed away and grabbed the cross, raising it and waving it between him and the tattooed warrior. "I absolve you. In the name of the Father, Son and Holy Spirit." He set down the cross, picked up the bowl, and flicked holy water onto Jarl, who grimaced and wiped it off.

"What is that?" Fenrir bent to ask me.

"Holy water," I whisper back. "It is meant to symbolize washing away his sins."

"Better use all of it," Fenrir muttered.

"Now," the priest turned to me and his tone softened, "Will you confess your sins, child?"

"No." Fenrir said, stepping in front of me, blocking the priest from getting closer. "She has already confessed."

"And been absolved," Jarl added. His smirk made heat roll through me, from my head to my toes.

"I have confessed, Father," I reassured the friar.

"It did not take as long. She sins a lot less," Jarl said.

The friar sighed. He turned his back and took up the chalice and ciborium, and began to mutter in Latin.

"What is he doing?"

"He's performing the sacrament," I whispered. We waited for the priest to finish. He consecrated the host and held the chalice and plate up over his head, then turned almost reluctantly to us.

He offered the goblet to Jarl while droning a line of Latin.

"The blood of the new covenant," I translated.

"Blood?" Jarl snarled. He took the cup and sniffed.

"Yes, the blood of our Lord Jesus, who died for our sins," the priest babbled.

Stay calm, I willed him silently. *Do not anger these men.* Jarl and Fenrir would not hurt me, but they wouldn't hesitate to slit this man's throat and find another priest.

"Doesn't smell like blood." Jarl sounded more curious than disgusted. He took a sip. I took the cup from him before he could drink more.

"And this is the body of Christ, given unto you," the priest went on hurriedly, offering the ciborium that held the host.

"The body? Do you mean flesh?" Jarl's voice was thick with a growl. "You eat the flesh of your god?"

"And you think we are heathens," Fenrir muttered to me.

The priest was squawking something. I took the Host and shoved it into Jarl's mouth. He startled but let me feed him. He even licked the crumbs from my fingers until my inner muscles twinged.

I pushed him back so I could take my part of the Host. Before I could hand the goblet back to the priest, Fenrir grabbed it and drained it down.

"Wine," he said dismissively, tossing the goblet to the ground. "Blood tastes different."

I closed my eyes.

The friar spoke the rest of the ceremony in double time, barely stopping to coach us through our vows. I'd not attended many weddings, but I was sure he'd left large chunks out. Perhaps the Berserkers' glinting weapons distracted him.

Finally he waved the cross in front of us and sprinkled us both with holy water for good measure.

"It is done?" Jarl growled. "We are married?"

"Yes," the priest bobbed his head. "May the Lord bless and keep you—"

"Good," Jarl said and drew me close to finish the kiss he'd started in the grove. His big hands cupped my face, and he drank of my lips until I stood dazed. Jarl made sure I was steady on my feet, gave my forehead a last kiss. He stepped back and Fenrir took his place beside me.

"Now me," Fenrir said.

"What?" the priest looked back and forth between us, clearly confused.

"It's my turn. I wish to marry this woman. You will speak the rites."

The priest gasped and crossed himself.

My insides curdled. "Fenrir, no."

"Yes." He took my arm and pulled me to his side. "I want this, little wife."

The priest was still gaping at us. "Y-you would marry her, too?"

"Yes."

"But—" the priest's protest died in a gurgle as Jarl held a dagger to the priest's neck. "You will do it," he growled.

"Jarl, leave him alone," I ordered.

"Hush, Juliet," Jarl said. Still holding the weapon on the priest, Jarl loosened a leather bag from his belt. It bulged, similar to Fenrir's. He upturned it and let the gold coin flash in front of the priest.

"Jarl," I said. My new husband stepped back.

The priest straightened his cassock. The toe of his boot hit the pile of gold and it clinked. A long pause, then he sighed and straightened.

The priest first looked to me. "Are you willing?" he asked weakly.

My heart warmed. "Yes, Father, I am willing."

"All right. God forgive me, I'll do it." He waved us both before him, and soon I was repeating the vows, and I was married again.

10

Fenrir

OUR LITTLE BRIDE looked dazed as we led her from the tiny church. As soon as we left the clearing, I gripped the back of her neck and guided her back to the grove where I'd left my pack.

I leaned close to whisper, "This way, little wife." Though I wouldn't have thought it possible, her cheeks reddened even further.

When we reached the grove, she stumbled away from me, backing away until she stood in the patch of bluebells.

"Is this why we came all this way? So you could marry me like this?"

"Yes. Does it make you happy?"

"Yes, but—" Her brow wrinkled.

"You didn't have a choice," I said quickly. "We will not allow you to leave us. We will bind you to us in any way we can." I came to her side and took her braid, starting to undo it.

"All right." She rubbed her forehead.

Jarl loosened the straps around his shoulders and let his shield and axe thud to the ground.

I loosened the last of her braid, letting her hair tumble around her shoulders.

"Come here, little wife. Now," Jarl ordered. I gave her a little push toward him.

She floated to him, the folds of her dress dragging over the flowers and releasing their bouquet. He held a torc in his hand, a ring of braided silver and gold. I lifted her hair so he could fit it around her slender neck.

"You belong to us in every way," he told her as he collared her. "Do you understand?"

She nodded.

"There's no escape." He lifted her chin and kissed her. When he finished with her lips, I was waiting.

"Do you have the oil?" he asked.

"In the pack," I said. Poor little wife. She would soon learn how thoroughly we would claim her.

I walked her back to a tree. I'd already unbound my cock. It was easy enough to lift her off her feet, toss up her skirts, and find her slick folds. I rubbed her a moment until her eyes rolled back in bliss. Then I hitched her higher, and let her slide down on my length. She sighed as gravity tugged her down, forcing her to impale herself. I braced her against the tree trunk and drove my hips forward and back. She shook her head, her hair tumbling around my face.

"That's it. Take it," I hammered her harder, driving into her over and over. She was hot and tight and perfect. I let her cum once, shuddering against the trunk. Then again, with her body limp on mine and her head pressed into my shoulder.

"Good girl," I kissed the side of her neck and let her down. I didn't cum. Not yet. I was saving myself for her ass.

"My turn," Jarl said. He pushed me aside, handing me the vial of oil.

He bent Juliet over and had her hang onto the trunk, her cheek pressed against the bark as he took her from behind. "Ah, yes. My reward." He held her hips and glided in and out slowly.

I walked around and felt down between her legs. I touched the little swollen nubbin above her entrance, playing with it while Jarl rocked in and out of her. But this time I didn't let her cum.

"Change positions," I advised Jarl and he nodded, swiping a forearm over his brow. When he pulled out, his rod was hard and shiny with her juices. He hadn't cum yet either.

"Lie down on me," he ordered Juliet, drawing her down and clamping an arm around her back so she didn't have any choice. The position left room for me to pull up her dress and bare her bottom. For a moment I was distracted by the pale half moons. I ran my hand over the tender flesh, and cracked my palm against it, admiring the pink print.

"Ah, do that again," Jarl groaned. He had his hands inside Juliet's bodice, gripping her breasts and guiding her to ride him.

I spanked her slowly, my slaps growing in intensity.

"Whenever you spank her, she clenches on me," Jarl growled.

"Tip her forward." I poured oil in my palm. When Jarl pulled Juliet flush against his chest, her bottom cheeks parted. I stroked oil into the pale valley and found the tender crinkle of her bottom hole.

Juliet squealed. "What are you doing?"

"We are your mates. We will do what we wish with you."

"And we wish to give you great pleasure."

She wriggled, trying to get away. I spanked her harder. Jarl laughed like a madman, holding her hips down.

She growled and clawed at him and he only laughed harder, wrapping his arms around her small body.

I finished sliding my fingers up and down her rear cleft and pushed a finger into her bottom. Her ass was tight and searing hot. *So good.*

"I want to feel," Jarl said.

I nodded. He pulled her off him, holding her tight as if she might run.

"All fours." He propped her the way he wanted her and caught the vial when I tossed it to him. I helped hold Juliet down so he could oil her bottom hole.

"Ah yes, that's good," he sighed. "Tight enough to snap my finger off. How will we fit our cocks up there?"

"I have a few ideas," I said, but right now I couldn't think of any of them. My cock was so hard, it might burst. I couldn't wait any longer. I grabbed a handful of our little nun's hair and guided her mouth to my jutting rod. "Suck me now," I ordered. My cock bumped against her mouth and her lips parted automatically. "Good girl. Do a good job and I won't take your ass right here." I'd claim it properly when we were back in the lodge.

Juliet bobbed her head up and down, taking me down as far as she could. I held her hair out of her face and murmured encouragement, though she hardly needed more than the threat of us taking her ass.

All too soon, I was spurting down her throat. She sputtered but swallowed me down. I scooped the seed that trickled from her lips back into her mouth.

"Ah, well done, little wife."

Her eyes were hooded, her lips puffy from taking my cock. She'd never looked so beautiful.

Jarl lay back and had her ride him while I spanked her some more. He came with a roar and held her tight to his chest while I took out the metal bulb I'd had made. I coated it with oil and pressed it against her dark rosebud until her ass opened and she accepted it.

"How long must I wear this?" she asked, sitting up gingerly. Her face was redder than her spanked ass.

"Until we are back at the lodge. Then we will take turns fucking your ass until you learn to cum with your ass full of cock."

She shuddered. I tugged on the plug and pushed it back in until it was fully seated in her ass. I did it again and again, then reached down to see if she'd grown wet.

She was dripping.

"You are our wife. Our little one. We will never hurt you. But we will claim you thoroughly," I promised.

Then we spread her out on her back in the bluebells, and ate her cunny until she screamed.

~

Juliet

THE PLUG in my bottom felt huge and unwieldy the whole journey back to our lodge. My stride was awkward, and when Jarl and Fenrir took turns carrying me in their arms, I couldn't help shifting my position every so often. They smirked at me, and I blushed, knowing they could tell exactly what was making me uncomfortable.

My pussy still dripped with arousal and their seed. I'd been claimed thoroughly, fully, and in ways I never thought possible. The Berserkers had promised to master me, and they had.

I was married. The tightness in my chest had eased. I still felt hollow, but it was a good feeling. My insides had been scoured clean. If my heart was a garden, the deep roots of something poisonous had been ripped out, and now there was ample room to grow something new.

I dozed in Fenrir's arms on the final leg of our journey, and by the time we entered the lodge, I was awake but drowsy.

He set me on the bed and went to help Jarl build up the fire. I shifted onto my side, to ease the feeling of the plug in my ass. It no longer burned, but my hole stretched uneasily around it. Every once in a while I clenched and was reminded of everything that had happened this afternoon all over again.

"Come, Juliet." Fenrir stripped me of my dress and boots. I stood naked before him, my arms wrapped around my bare chest.

Fenrir drew me between his legs. I shifted from foot to foot, wishing the stretch of my bottom hole would ease.

"You're doing well, little wife. How do you feel?"

I shrugged. He stroked back the messy tendrils of my hair.

Jarl prowled up to the bed. "Do you admit you belong to us, now?"

I almost rolled my eyes at that. "If I say no, what would you do?"

"Tie you up again and whip you until you admit the

truth." His eyes gleamed and a hot jolt of arousal shot through me. The Berserkers had trained me to respond.

"I belong to you, as you belong to me." I raised my chin. "Husband."

Fenrir chuckled. "Well said, little wife." He tipped me over his lap, so my upturned bottom gave him perfect access to the plug. He plucked and pushed at it, moving it in and out. I kicked and struggled with each invasion, but my arousal grew.

"You still are our captive and our mate. But we meant the vows we spoke." Fenrir stroked my back as he used the plug to probe my ass. "We will be true to you, Juliet. We will love and protect you and cherish you forever." He spanked my bottom, his palm catching the plug and making me cry out as arousal bloomed hot and wild between my legs. I angled my hips, trying to rub against his leg. Fenrir saw my desperation and chuckled. He slapped my rear until each cheek glowed like a coal in the fire. Then he flipped me onto the bed, onto my back.

The position pushed the plug deeper inside me. I tried to roll off my back, but Jarl caught me and pulled me back, so I still lay on my back with my head on his lap. Fenrir knelt between my legs, pushing my knees wider and pinning them lightly with his weight. My legs were open, my cunny spread wide with pink folds dripping as the plug impaled my ass.

"We will still punish you. And we will claim you thoroughly," Fenrir promised. He set his palm against my cunny and ground down lightly. Sparks shot from my center, my arousal catching fire and starting to spread.

He lifted his hands and tapped his fingers against my folds, spanking lightly. My head flew back and I shuddered. Jarl smiled down at me, gripping my bare breast and kneading it. Between his touch and Fenrir's light slaps to my cunny, I felt like the sensation would tear me apart.

"You are ours, Juliet. You belong to us." Fenrir's hand fell harder now, in a steady rhythm like the beat of a drum. Each smack drove me onward, toward that glorious place where pleasure would consume me. I cried out, writhing and grinding down, seeking that bliss and the blow to my cunny that would send me flying. As I rooted myself in the bed, I impaled myself further on the plug.

And at last it caught, that wildfire. The flames spread and roared higher. Pleasure scorched me. I flew higher and higher, borne by the pleasure fueled by pain. My climax burned white hot, obliterating me.

Strong hands caught my trembling body, bearing me back to earth. I found myself on my belly. As I scrambled up to hands and knees, Jarl cupped my face and crooned to me. Fenrir gripped my hips, stilling me. He pulled my lower half back against him until the iron hard muscle of his legs pressed against the backs of my thighs. The crisp hairs around his cock brushed my bottom.

"It is time." His hands parted my bottom cheeks. He shifted me forward so there was space and then, with a hand on my belly to steady me, he drew out the plug.

I groaned as the widest part of the bulb stretched me. Then my bottom was empty, my hole clenching on air only for a moment before Fenrir inserted his hard fingers. He stretched me further and he must have used the oil, because it dripped down the backs of my thighs. My empty cunny prickled with need.

"I'm going to claim your arse, little nun," Fenrir murmured, his fingers thrusting into my bottom hole in a shameful rhythm. I moaned and dropped my forehead to the bed. Jarl gathered my hair back and stroked my scalp in soothing circles. Tingles spread up my spine, my body clenching in anticipation.

"I'm going to master you fully. From the moment we found you in the abbey, I have wanted to claim you like this," Fenrir kept fucking me with his fingers as he whispered. "If I had my way, I would've spread you out on the lawn and claimed you then, naked before your God and all the world."

I whimpered against the surge of arousal spurred by his words.

"Imagine the torches burning all around," he continued. "Imagine the moon bearing witness to your shame and your pleasure." His fingers slid from my ass, replaced by the hard tip of his cock. He was bigger than the plug. Oh God, how could I bear it?

"Bear down, Juliet," Jarl ordered. "Push out and let him in." His fingers reached under my chest to pluck my nipples. "Do it and we will let you cum."

I did as he bid, moaning as Fenrir slid inside. I felt pleasure churning deep in my belly even as my bottom hole stretched to its limits. Sweat slicked my back.

Fenrir growled and cursed as he pushed in further, seating himself deep inside me. Someone, either Jarl or Fenrir, reached under me and played with the slippery folds of my cunny. Pleasure shot through me and I screamed, clenching down hard on his cock.

Fenrir shouted and bucked, spearing me fully. The sensation spurred my climax to new heights. Fenrir eased out and slid back in, driving me forward onto the bed.

Jarl lifted my head by my hair and cupped my jaw, guiding his cock into my mouth. "Suck me now, little nun. Take us both."

I hummed around his rod, my tongue rubbing along the

heated skin. I sucked hard, drawing him deep, even as my bottom swallowed Fenrir's cock further.

"That's it," Fenrir murmured. His hand pressed on my back, making me arch further. My head tipped back and Jarl slid his cock deeper into my throat. "That's the way."

I breathed through my nose, scenting Jarl's wild musk as the hairs around his cock tickled my face. Meanwhile, Fenrir fucked my ass in slow, easy drags. I should not feel pleasure, but I did, deep down. Sensation and shame twisting together to make pleasure of the darkest kind.

"You are so beautiful, Juliet," Fenrir said. "So beautiful and so good, to take my cock up your ass so well."

His crude words made me clench my inner muscles, hard. Jarl gripped my hair tighter, holding me still.

"Oh gods, yes," Fenrir muttered, sounding drunk. "Do that again."

I angled my head so I could breath more easily. Jarl slid out and smacked his cock on my cheek before gliding back in. My mouth watered as it filled with his thick meat.

Fenrir reached under and rubbed my folds with no gentleness or precision. My climax gripped and shook me, and my bottom squeezed and squeezed Fenrir's cock until he came, shuddering against me.

I panted, drooling around Jarl's rod. I'd cum with a cock in my ass and cum hard. Fenrir drew out of me, slowly. Where I once felt stretched, I now felt empty.

Jarl pulled out of my mouth, still hard. "My turn."

Fenrir took his place by my head. "You're doing well." His fingers trailed lazily from my breasts to the sensitive nub near my entrance. "Cum for me again."

I fought it, but Fenrir knew just where to rub and where to pinch. I wriggled until Jarl pushed inside my ass, spearing me and holding me still.

He cursed loud and long. "She's so tight and hot," he said.

"She is," Fenrir answered, still rubbing my folds. "And when she cums—"

"She clenches hard enough to snap off my cock." Jarl's finger dug into my hips as he rolled his hips, surging deeper into my bowels.

Fenrir stroked me, his fingers barely a whisper over my skin, achingly sweet. Jarl's cock was a battering ram, pounding me toward climax. Together, their assault overwhelmed me. My orgasm lifted my body up and threw it into the abyss.

11

Juliet

Warm, wet cloths stroked over my skin. Jarl and Fenrir cleaned me with a care and thoroughness that made me flush. They rubbed balm into my sore spots, including my poor, stretched bottom.

Finally, Fenrir gathered me against him. His hand slipped between my legs.

"Oh no." I tried to roll away, but he held me fast.

"Yes, little wife. One last time."

"I can't, I can't," I moaned.

"You must." His thumb rubbed gently, pushing me over the edge. I shuddered and curled into him, pressing my face into the hard plane of muscle. He took his hand away and replaced it with a wet cloth, pressing down and grounding me.

Once he'd cleaned me, I curled further into myself. I felt small and fragile, completely wrung out.

Fenrir curled his big body around me. His chin rested atop my head, his arms and legs lay along mine. I'd never felt so safe or protected.

Pleasure had wracked my body, destroying me. The old Juliet, the hardened shell I'd created to keep me hidden from the world, was obliterated.

But the real Juliet, the essence of myself, was not dead. She lived.

For so many years, the real part of me had been sleeping. Now she was waking slowly, a sprout pushing through the dark earth. Most of my life I kept myself hidden safe in the warm, loving embrace of the darkness. Soon I'd unfurl and raise my head to the sun.

But that could come later. For now, I'd sleep, curled up and protected by the giant Berserker. My husband, my captor, my mate.

I woke in the darkness. Fenrir had left the bed and stood by the door. Moonlight spilled inside, shimmering down the waterfall of Fenrir's hair, caressing the dark markings running down Jarl's bare arms.

I caught their murmurs but could not make out the words or their meanings. I could guess, though. Jarl had kept watch, and now it was Fenrir's turn. I did not know why they were keeping watch now. My head was fuzzy with sleep, so when Jarl returned to bed, I had thoughts only for Jarl, coming to lie with me.

My husband.

I uncurled and opened my arms to him. He grabbed a fur robe and in one move dropped onto the bed and rolled over me, and kept rolling until I was wrapped in the fur, bound against him.

"Juliet." His breath caressed my face. I wriggled deeper into the robe, and so writhed against him. His breath caught and his cock grew against my leg. I stifled a giggle.

"Are you sore?" he whispered. I took a moment to listen to my body. My bottom hole felt worn but the rest of me shimmered with eagerness.

"I ache," I told him honestly. "But I ache for you."

I felt him draw back, as if he tried to gauge my expression in the darkness.

"Truly?" Then his hand found my folds, and discovered the truth.

"Love me," I invited, opening to my legs to him.

"Juliet," he sighed, and guided his length into my waiting entrance.

I tightened my hold on his shoulders. "Take me. Don't hold back."

He thrust into me, clamping me close as his hips worked his cock deep. His lips found mine and his tongue surged inside, claiming my mouth as his cock claimed my warm cunny. Pleasure washed through me, not hard and wild like before, but easy and gentle as spring rain. Jarl finished with a shudder. He loosened his hold around me but made no move to slip from my body.

For a moment we simply held each other, face to face in the dark. He dipped his head to nuzzle at my temple.

"There is no god, no goddess, nothing holy or magic for me but you," he whispered.

"Don't say that." I covered his mouth with my hands. "Don't blaspheme."

He looked at me under his dark brows and long eyelashes and moved his lips under my palms. "It's how I feel." He pulled my hands away and kissed my lips, gently. "This is sacred." He tugged the robe around us, cocooning me in warmth. His cock was still hard inside me, but it felt right. We fit.

My eyes drooped and I fell asleep with his cock deep inside me and his whisper echoing in my ear. "As long as I live, I will worship at your altar."

∽

IN THE MORNING, I rose to a warm but empty lodge. I sat up and took stock of myself. Two arms, two legs, two well-used holes. One heart, happy and full.

I found water and cleansed then dressed myself. In my mind's eye, Jarl and Fenrir burned like bright stars. My husbands were outside, chopping wood and stacking it in rows against the lodge. I sent a pulse of love down the mental tether, and busied myself plucking the partridges they'd brought in as game.

It was a morning like any other, yet everything had changed. Jarl and Fenrir came in one by one, with logs to feed the fire. They kissed me and took their kill to spit and roast it. When the meat was cooked, we shared a horn of mead and broke our fast.

We didn't speak. We didn't need to. This was a morning I'd always wanted and never dared to dream of—me and my husbands together, working and eating and sitting side by side. Soon we would rise and wash out hands and go outside to work and play in the fresh air. Whatever the day held we would face it together.

Fenrir finished first and brought a bowl of water to me. I washed the grease from my fingers, and when I was done, he set the bowl aside for Jarl.

"Juliet," he said as he caught my face between his hands. "Are you happy with us?"

As if he could not feel what was in my heart. "I am."

"Good." He kissed either of my cheeks, my forehead, and finally my lips. "Remember that, and the pleasure we gave you." With that confusing statement, Fenrir stepped away and Jarl took his place.

My tattooed husband bent to kiss my lips. "For us, one smile from you is worth the world." He tweaked my chin. "And one moment with you is worth risking death."

Death? I wanted to ask what he meant. Both warriors looked so serious, my heart stopped.

Before I could speak, a shout went up outside the lodge.

"Stay here, Juliet." As one, Jarl and Fenrir turned. They marched side by side to the door of the lodge and opened it.

A host of warriors stood in the clearing. Fenrir and Jarl went out of the door, blocking my view. I scrambled to put on my boots, but I heard the lead Berserker clearly.

"Fenrir and Jarl, you're wanted for kidnapping a spaewife. Do you yield?"

"We yield," Fenrir said quietly. He and Jarl stepped away from the lodge, their hands outstretched at their sides to show they held no weapons.

"You will come with us now," the warrior ordered. He motioned and a group of Berserkers, bristling with weapons, stepped forward and surrounded my husbands.

What was happening?

"Wait," I called, stumbling out with my right boot half on.

"Juliet," a warrior called, loping to my side. He was big and blond and looked familiar. Hazel's mate. "I am Knut. Hazel made me come. She is heavy with child, but insisted she would make the climb unless I promised to find you."

"What is happening?" I reached down and tugged my boot on properly.

"They broke the Alphas' decree and kidnapped a spaewife," Knut said. "There is to be a trial."

"What? Which spaewife?"

His blond brows pulled together and I realized he meant me. I was the spaewife they'd stolen.

This was all wrong. The warriors were herding Jarl and Fenrir away.

"Wait," I cried. "You cannot do this!"

"Stay back, little wife," Fenrir called. At his side, Jarl hunched, his whole body heaving. The warriors made a circle around him, their weapons pointed inwards. Jarl was close to the Change.

He needs you to be safe. That is the only way he will keep control. Fenrir spoke into my mind.

I froze.

Knut stepped forward and addressed my husbands. "She will not come to harm. I swear it."

With a nod, Fenrir gripped Jarl's shoulder and hauled him back. The troop of warriors marched them down the path.

I wanted to rush after them, but Knut blocked my path. The scarred warrior who led the troop of warriors stood near, waiting to bring up the rear.

"Where are you taking them?" I asked him.

"To the Alphas," the scarred warrior answered. He looked grave. He nodded to Knut and followed his warriors down the path.

It's all right, Juliet. It will be all right, Fenrir whispered into my mind.

But it was not all right. Nothing was.

I startled when Knut dropped a fur cloak over my shoulders. "Shhh," he said. "Juliet, you're safe now."

The fur cloak held the scent of my warriors. I drew it

around me, welcoming the warmth. "I don't understand what is happening."

"The warriors Jarl and Fenrir took you without permission," Knut said. "They have broken the Alphas' law."

"What law?" I asked before I remembered. I covered my mouth with my hands when I remembered what Fenrir had told me, long ago. *"The penalty for touching a spaewife is death."*

"Is that what's happening? They will be put to death for claiming me?"

"The law is very clear," Knut said, adding in a gentler tone, "Are you hurt? Did they hurt you?"

"No," I brushed him off. "They did not hurt me." They healed me. They gave me everything I wanted. "I need to see them."

He shook his head. "That cannot happen."

"They are my husbands," I snapped. He blinked at me, his brow furrowing. "My mates. I belong with them." Panic flared in me. "You cannot put them to death. I need them."

He rubbed his blond beard. "There will be a trial before the Alphas and the Gathering. Jarl and Fenrir will be sentenced then."

I was breathless as if I had raced up a mountain. "Then take me to the Alphas."

Knut frowned at me and I stomped my foot, my voice ringing out. "Now!"

~

KNUT DID NOT TAKE me to Jarl and Fenrir or the Alphas. Instead, I found myself in a mountain cave, pacing back and forth. The cave was clean and well appointed, with finely carved wooden chairs and chests, tapestries, and an iron stand that held a small fire. Brenna's Alphas made their home in caves such as these. I was too agitated to sit.

Murmurs echoed down the hall, and two women pushed the curtain aside and entered the room. The dim firelight shone on their faces. One was dark and the other fair, and I recognized them from the few times I'd seen them from afar. Muriel and Sabine.

My mouth was too dry to speak, but Sabine, the tall blonde, merely looked me up and down with unnerving perusal. Her sister Muriel spoke first. "Sister Juliet."

"Just Juliet," I said automatically. "I am no longer a nun."

"Juliet, then." Her voice was warm, compassionate. "How are you?"

I found myself speechless again. I had been through so much. "Physically, I am well," I stammered.

"Good." She swept her hand to a chair. "Please, sit."

"I don't want to sit. I wish to speak to the Alphas." I moved to the door, but Sabine was blocking it.

"We have been sent to care for you."

I drew myself up, though I was no match for her height. "I do not need anyone to care for me," I snapped. "I was fine, I did not need a rescue—" I cut myself off with a hand to my mouth. I was almost shouting. "I wish to see Jarl and Fenrir. I need to know they have not come to harm."

"They have not been harmed," Muriel said. I turned to her.

"How do you know?"

"My mate Wulfgar was the one who brought them back from their lodge. He told me. Jarl and Fenrir are well, though they are still under guard." Muriel seated herself gracefully in a gilt chair. "Please."

I sat. My sigh gusted out and made the flames gutter.

"There will be a trial," Sabine said. Her voice echoed

oddly in the small space. "The warriors will be called to account for what they did to you."

"What they did to me?" I repeated. "What is it they are said to have done?" I clasped my hands in my lap to keep them from shaking.

"They stole you and kept you hidden on the far side of the mountain. The blizzard kept us from searching for you."

"Be assured, Juliet. You are safe now," Muriel said. And then the pity in her eyes made sense.

"You think they kidnapped me. Took me against my will."

"Did they not?" Sabine twitched her head to the side. Her eyes were almost black in the lowlight.

"I..." How to explain? I could not lie. "They came across me when I suffered from the mating fever." I glanced up at Muriel and she gave an encouraging nod. "I was hiding as best I could, but they knew. And they wanted to ease my suffering." I threaded my fingers tighter. "They helped me."

"Did they take you against your will?" Sabine asked.

"They wished to help me. And they did. My fever is gone."

"They did not get permission from the Alphas," Sabine swept past me to add a few pieces of wood to the fire. "The rules are in place for a reason. We cannot allow warriors to simply claim whom they will."

"From my understanding, that is exactly what the Berserkers have done. How else will you explain the night they sacked the abbey and carried us off?"

"That was for your protection," Sabine said.

"It is true, many spaewives found their mates that night," Muriel said. "But this is different. The Alphas have decreed—"

"But once a spaewife comes into heat, she is able to choose a mate, correct?"

"Yes," Muriel said slowly. "But Juliet—"

"Well, I have chosen." I crossed my arms and jutted out my chin.

"Truly? You were a nun." Sabine also crossed her arms over her chest.

"I am no longer. Jarl and Fenrir are my husbands. I married them in a church. A priest oversaw our vows."

Sabine blinked. Muriel leaned forward. "They took you to a priest?"

"Yes."

"And you married them?" Sabine asked.

"Yes." I groaned and covered my face with my hands. "Both of them. They made the priest do it."

Sabine and Muriel exchanged glances. Sabine's eyebrows climbed toward her hairline. "Truly? The priest married you? Twice? To two different men?"

"It wasn't like he wanted to do it." I rubbed my forehead. "The warriors would've killed him."

Sabine snickered. Muriel poked her.

"We will speak to the Alphas," Muriel assured me. "They will listen to your side of things."

"Thank you." I sagged in my seat.

"Have no fear." Muriel took my hand. "It will be well."

Sabine's head was bowed and her eyes closed. I hoped she was relaying the information to her Alpha mates.

I turned to Muriel. "Tell me of the girls. All the spaewives. How is everyone?"

"They are well." Muriel's face brightened. "Laurel had her baby. A son. Looks just like his father."

"Which one?" I asked.

"Ulfarr. The one who was scarred in a fire."

Sabine raised her head. For a moment, her eyes glinted with a bright yellow light.

"Hazel will give birth next," she said with calm assurance. I wanted to ask how she knew, but bit my tongue. I knew she was an herbalist and was training with witches to learn their craft. It seemed she also was learning the midwife arts.

"I want to be there," I said. I had wanted to be there for Laurel's birth, but had stayed away because of the fever. "That is, if she'll have me."

"Of course she'll have you," Muriel said. "You are the closest to a mother the orphans have known. And there are plenty more babies coming. We will be busy this spring."

"And summer. And fall," Sabine added with a sly arch of her brow.

Muriel blushed and put a hand to her belly.

"The unmated spaewives—the girls," I asked. "Are they well?"

A shadow crossed Sabine's face. "We have moved them to the Alphas' cave where they are easier to guard."

Oh dear. I did not like to hear that the girls had been uprooted again. "Is that because Jarl and Fenrir took me? Because—"

"No," Sabine cut me off. "It's not because you were stolen. There are fewer warriors available to guard because we are at war with the Corpse King."

The breath left my chest. "We are?"

"We must move against him, soon," Muriel's brow furrowed as she looked to her sister for confirmation. "The witches have decided."

"Why now?" I twisted the folds of my gown in my fingers.

"We think he might have more power soon," Sabine said

grimly. She looked different, somehow, more remote, the sharp planes of her figure cut from shadow. "We must fight him before it's too late and he cannot be stopped."

"More power?" I breathed. "How?"

There was a pause and Muriel said, "Rosalind woke."

"She's all right?" Rosalind had sustained a head wound and been unconscious for days.

"She is gone. Somehow, she woke and fled the mountain. Wulfgar says he doesn't know how she slipped through the guards again." Muriel bit her lip.

"We believe she is in league with the Corpse King," Sabine said.

"That's impossible." I wracked my memory. All those times Rosalind was angry and brooding. She hated the Berserkers and hated her fate.

Perhaps it was possible.

"There's no way she slipped away without help. And Sorrel told us why Rosalind left the first time. She was trying to aid the Corpse King."

I covered my mouth with my hand. *Oh Rosalind, what have you done?*

"It's all right," Muriel patted my hand. "All will be well."

"Sister Juliet," a warrior was at the door. I rose, smoothing down my dress. "The Alphas are ready for you."

12

Juliet

I FOLLOWED the warrior down the mountain path to the place of the standing stones. Sabine and Muriel came with me, and for that I was glad, or as glad as I could be under the circumstances.

A great crowd of warriors had assembled in the clearing. Some stalked as wolves through the crowd. As I stepped into their ranks, a path formed, and I followed it to the fires and the great stones where the Alphas sat. Each footstep I took was matched by the beat of the drums. My own heart fluttered wildly out of time, but when I came to my place, I composed my face. I would remain calm.

Jarl and Fenrir stood to the side; their hands bound in front of them. I felt their gaze flit over me, and the featherlight mental touch of their minds to mine. Checking to see I was unhurt.

The drums boomed louder, their rhythm faster, and the Alphas filed in. I fisted my hands at my sides.

I could do this.

The largest warrior, a blond with a great beard, sat on a stone throne. This was Samuel, one of Brenna's mates. He gazed around the clearing and the drums fell silent. After a moment, he began.

"We are gathered here for the trial of Jarl and Fenrir. These warriors have broken our decree and harmed a spaewife. They took her for their own and held her in a hidden lodge for several days. They do not deny it." Though he spoke in a low, measured tone, his voice boomed around the clearing, amplified by the stones. "Will anyone speak for them?"

I stepped forward before I began. "I am Juliet, and I will speak for them."

"You will?" asked Samuel. "Why?"

"They are my husbands." I was shaking, but I shouted louder. "In the eyes of God and man."

The Alpha cocked his head to the side. "Which god?"

"My God. They knew I kept the faith, and they sought a priest so we could be married. They have treated me well. And though I was reluctant at first," the corner of my mouth quirked at the understated truth, "I am their wife now. I will not leave them."

"So you accept these men as your mates?"

"Yes. My mates and my husbands. I wish that you would pardon them." My voice broke but I forged on. "I love them."

Across the fire, Jarl and Fenrir held my gaze.

"Is this true?" Samuel looked beyond me. "She has accepted them?"

"It's true." Muriel and Sabine stepped to my side. "We have spoken with Juliet and she told us everything."

Samuel thought some more. The assembly of warriors was quiet, almost too quiet. I knew Samuel was communing with his Alpha brothers, but I did not know what the verdict would be.

Overhead, hawks wheeled in the spring sunshine. My legs trembled.

"Very well." When Samuel spoke up again, I nearly toppled over. I gripped my skirts harder. "Spaewife Juliet, we hear your plea." His voice softened. "Because you have spoken for them, we will not sentence them to death. But we cannot overlook their crime. There are consequences to kidnapping and keeping a spaewife." He glared at the assembled warriors.

"Didn't they do what you did?" My voice rang out before I could stop it. Samuel looked to me and I wiped my sweating palms on my gown. "My lord, forgive me. But we've all heard the stories of how you found your mate. And how the Alphas of the Lowland pack found theirs."

A murmur rose among the warriors. "Silence," Ragnvald ordered and fixed me with a crooked grin. "You know the tales, so you know why there are rules. You know why they are important. We must protect the spaewives."

"They did protect me." From myself. "But if you will hold them to rules you yourself broke, then I pray you will show them mercy."

"Mercy," Samuel murmured, stroking his blond beard. Beside him, on a smaller stone throne, Brenna reached out and squeezed his hand.

"Very well. We will show them mercy. But they will still have a punishment. In the coming war with the Corpse King, they will fight on the front lines."

I covered my face with my hands.

Muriel put her hand on my back in comfort. "At least it is not a death sentence."

"Is it not?" I muttered. The Corpse King's magic was growing. The witches did not dare approach him, lest he conquer them and drain their powers for his own. How would the Berserkers fare?

Muriel moved away, and the scent of woodsmoke surrounded me. "It's all right, little wife," Fenrir tugged my hands down. I threw myself against him, hugging him, soaking in his warmth.

Jarl pressed against my back. "We will fight and we will win."

"They say it's hopeless," I whispered.

"Then you must pray. You have told us stories of your God and his followers. Didn't they often face the impossible?"

"Yes." I blink as Jarl brushed tears off my cheeks.

"Then pray to your God. And believe."

∾

Juliet

THE MOON WAS WAXING ONCE MORE when I stood again in the door of the lodge Jarl and Fenrir had built for me. My hands rubbed the curve of my belly. I was not showing, but one day my belly would be as round as the full moon. I had not told anyone, because they would insist I stay in the Alphas' caves with the rest of the women.

I paced in front of the lodge, unable to keep still. Today was the day the Berserkers were returning home. My men had fought on the front lines, and though I'd heard reports that they were well, I would not believe it until I laid my eyes on them.

My faith only stretched so far.

Please, I begged, lifting my face to the moon. I had prayed to God every day, and kept busy tending to the orphans. And though waiting was hard, a peace had fallen over me.

The time for waiting was over.

Juliet? Where are you? I nearly leapt at the touch of Fenrir's mind to mine.

I am here. I sent him an image of myself standing in the doorway of the lodge. *I am waiting.* I stopped pacing. I shifted from foot to foot, my heart pounding like a drum.

We are coming. We are almost home.

I closed my eyes and Saw what surrounded my warriors. The path up the mountain. Around them, the forest blurred.

I opened my eyes the exact moment Jarl's head appeared over the rise. Fenrir followed. When they saw me, they quickened their pace, only to slow as they approached. They looked tired, and their clothes were dirty, but they were home.

I raced the final steps to them, grabbed the front of their jerkins and pulled them down to kiss them both.

"Thank God. Thank God." I was sobbing.

"Thank Fenrir. He saved my life more than once." Jarl grunted.

"Thank you," I breathed and launched myself into Fenrir's arms. He laughed as he caught me.

"Is it over?" I asked. "Is it done?"

He pressed his forehead to mine. "It's done. The mountain is safe."

I did not ask how they defeated the Corpse King. That

story would come, perhaps when we were back at the mouth to the Alphas' caves, gathered around the fire.

"Little wife," Fenrir cupped my face in his hands and looked me over. When he got to my feet, he frowned. "Where are your boots?"

I laughed through my tears. "I gave them to Meadow." The oldest of the unmated spaewives had been pining since all available warriors were called to fight the Corpse King. A new pair of boots gave her some cheer.

A growl rumbled in Fenrir's chest as he wiped my tears away. He shook his head, mock grumbling, "As soon as we bring them to you, you give them away."

"Meadow thanks you for the gift." I closed my eyes as he nuzzled my cheek, giving the side of my neck a little nip. "I did it so you would return safely to me."

When he stood back from me, he had a pair of new boots in his hands. "Do not give these away. Simply tell us who needs a pair, and we will provide for them."

"Thank you, husband."

"Let's go inside," he growled. "It's too cold for you."

I sighed and let him draw me back near the fire. "The weather is still not right for late spring." I bit my lip. Was it fallout from the Corpse King?

"It may take time for the weather to return to normal," Fenrir said. "But do not fear, little mother. We fully enjoy the time we pass indoors."

They laid me down and fussed over me. Fenrir tucked me into the pelts while Jarl built up the fire.

"There's plenty of wood," he remarked.

"Knut kept it stocked," I said from my place, cozy and warm in the furs. "He brought me here today, in gratitude for helping his mate. Hazel gave birth at the time of the new moon. A girl."

"Knut is a father." Fenrir shook his head.

I ducked my head. By Michaelmas, they too would be fathers, but I had not told them.

As they completed their chores one by one, they left to dip in the cold stream that ran beside the lodge. They returned, naked and tossing their heads to shake off the excess water. The sight of their bare bodies warmed me through and through.

"It's good to be clean," Fenrir said, and Jarl agreed.

"We brought some fresh game," Jarl opened his pack. "We also have dried meat, though I am sick of it."

"We can hunt," Fenrir added.

"I am not hungry for meat," I told them. "I am hungry for you." I tossed away the pelt covering me and pulled up my dress.

The bed shook as two Berserkers lay down. "Little wife," Jarl growled against my lips. "We are hungry for you as well."

I kissed him until my face was red and chafed from his thick beard. When I turned to Fenrir, Jarl set his hands inside my dress bodice and ripped it open.

I gasped and he muttered, "We'll find you another."

Fenrir claimed my mouth as Jarl browsed between my breasts. His teeth latched onto my sensitive nipple and I cried out.

Fenrir raised his head. "Are you all right?"

"Yes." I grabbed Jarl's head and pulled him closer. "More. I want more."

My husbands ripped away the rest of my dress as they worked their way down. They turned me on my side between them, Jarl at the front, Fenrir at the back. Their beards scratched my skin as they kissed me, nuzzling and breathing in my scent.

Jarl hooked my left leg over his shoulder and nosed close to my aching entrance. Fenrir left the bed for a moment. When he returned, he drizzled oil along my backside. His fingers delved between my cheeks as Jarl's tongue flicked over my folds. My hips rocked back and forth as both men fucked me, one with his fingers, the other with his tongue. My orgasm dashed over me like a shock of fresh water. The lodge filled with my breathy cries.

"Naughty wife," Fenrir murmured against my shoulder. He pressed his big body against mine, rubbing his cock against the back of my leg. "What is it you want?"

"You," I whispered. *I want you*, I added, speaking into the channel that linked our minds. I shared the image of me strung up between the frame with arms above my head and legs wide. My body glistened with oil in the firelight.

"Tie me up," I murmured. "Punish me. I want to feel you."

"You wish to be punished?" Jarl ground the palm of his hand against my folds, sparking new pleasure.

"Yes." I rocked my hips harder, but Jarl took his hand away.

"What about the child?" Fenrir placed his hand on my belly. "When were you going to tell us?"

I bit my lip. "I thought you might guess."

Fenrir rolled me to my back gently, and planted a kiss on my still flat belly. "We knew as soon as we scented you."

"Your scent is different," Jarl said. He stood beside the bed with leather ties in his hand. "Well, brother, how shall we punish her for keeping secrets?"

"We tie her up and claim her fully," Fenrir said and drew me to my feet. He tugged the torc around my neck, then clamped his hand on the back of my neck and marched me to the frame where Jarl waited. As they moved me into position, the Berserkers were gentle but the gleam in their eyes made me shiver.

Jarl tied my arms above my head while Fenrir secured my feet. Then they ran their hands over me, stroking and oiling every part of me thoroughly. I rolled my hips forward, begging, but Jarl kept his touch brisk. All too soon they took their hands away.

Fenrir clapped his hand against my bottom. He spanked one side then the other while Jarl stood before me, gliding his oiled hand along his cock. I arched my back, pushing out my breasts to entice him. Jarl smirked and shook his head.

When Fenrir finished and stepped back, my bottom was warm.

"Breathe," Jarl told me, and I didn't understand. Fenrir braided my hair and placed it over my shoulder so it hung down my front. He stepped back and my skin prickled. The next instant, a stinging rain struck between my shoulders. I cried out.

"Breathe," Jarl reminded me. He placed a hand over my heart. "Just breathe."

The knotted ends of the flogger struck again. Fenrir painted my back with crisp strokes. The strands bit again and again. When he stopped and pressed his body to my back, I cried out and struggled as the hair on his chest abraded my sensitive skin. My cunny throbbed with a delicious ache. Each pulse was bigger than the last, pulling me under.

I heard the wild and pagan beat, deep in my mind, pounding with the rhythm of my heart. The drums. They were a part of me.

Jarl stepped forward, his naked body caressed in moonlight and flame. His tattoos writhed across his chest like dark demonic tongues. He stood in front of me and tugged my head back by my braid. As he kissed me, he slid his cock inside. My inner muscles fluttered as he worked his cock fully into my tight channel. When my body opened and accepted him fully, we both groaned.

Jarl fucked me slowly. Every time Jarl drew out, Fenrir flogged me again, snapping the leather strands against my bottom until heat flooded my sex. He bent and untied my feet, and I twined my legs around Jarl, pulling him close.

"You are so tight," Jarl growled. "How do you feel?"

"Full." When he thrust deep, I felt him in every part of me.

"Not full enough." Fenrir drizzled my oil down my crack. Jarl hitched me higher against him, and Fenrir set the firm bulb of the plug against my ass.

"Oh no," I moaned.

"Oh yes." Fenrir pushed until the plug stretched my bottom hole. Jarl came, groaning against my shoulder. "Feel this, brother." He stepped away, and Fenrir took his place.

Fenrir took me harder, slamming deep enough to make the plug vibrate in my bottom. He jerked his hips up in short, pulsing bursts that made my eyes roll back in my head. Pleasure tightened in a golden coil in my lower belly, sensation spiraling upwards.

At my back, Jarl's teeth scraped my shoulder. He pulled out the bulb, leaving my bottom hole empty and gaping. I cried out, my fingers flexing in the bindings. Jarl worked his cock inside my ass, inch by inch, while I pleaded for mercy.

When my orgasm exploded, it sent me soaring. I floated above the frame, watching myself writhe between the two warriors as they worked their cocks into my small body.

I was bound between them. Tied up and at their mercy. My body was caged, but my heart was free.

"We worship you," Fenrir whispered in my ear. He

surged in deep, slamming me further onto Jarl's rod. I came back into my body with a cry. Sweat ran down my chest and disappeared between us. "Little goddess."

I was too overwhelmed to protest. I gripped the leather bindings and pulled myself up higher between them. Fenrir held my hips still as Jarl scythed in and out of my tight rear channel. Everything in me drew up, tightened to the breaking point, building to climax.

Fenrir began to fuck me with deep, plowing thrusts. I trembled and cried out, overcome. My climax grew, a white hot bloom big as the moon.

Pleasure exploded, filling me with light.

Juliet, my husbands cried, sharing my climax. I felt them but was too far away to answer. I rose to a place beyond thought, beyond flesh. I was lost in a world of sensation, where nothing existed. There was no God, no man, nothing but bliss. I was not Juliet. I was the purest version of myself, a spirit, pure light. And Jarl and Fenrir were with me, but there were no boundaries between us.

We were one.

FREE BOOK

Get a secret Berserker book, Bred by the Berserkers (only to the awesomesauce fans on Lee's email list)
Click here to get started...https://geni.us/BredBerserker

WANT MORE BERSERKERS?

These fierce warriors will stop at nothing to claim their mates…

The Berserker Saga

Sold to the Berserkers - – Brenna, Samuel & Daegan
Mated to the Berserkers - – Brenna, Samuel & Daegan
Bred by the Berserkers (FREE novella only available at www.leesavino.com) - – Brenna, Samuel & Daegan
Taken by the Berserkers – Sabine, Ragnvald & Maddox
Given to the Berserkers – Muriel and her mates
Claimed by the Berserkers – Fleur and her mates

Berserker Brides

Rescued by the Berserker – Hazel & Knut
Captured by the Berserkers – Willow, Leif & Brokk
Kidnapped by the Berserkers – Sage, Thorbjorn & Rolf
Bonded to the Berserkers – Laurel, Haakon & Ulf

Berserker Babies – the sisters Brenna, Sabine, Muriel, Fleur and their mates
Night of the Berserkers – the witch Yseult's story
Owned by the Berserkers – Fern, Dagg & Svein
Tamed by the Berserkers — Sorrel, Thorsteinn & Vik

Berserker Warriors

Ægir *(formerly titled The Sea Wolf)*
Siebold

ALSO BY LEE SAVINO

Paranormal Romance

Draekons (menage dragons) with Lili Zander and Draekon Rebel Force. Start with Draekon Warrior.

Bad Boy Alphas with Renee Rose (bad boy werewolves) - start with Alpha's Temptation.

Contemporary Romance

Royally Fake Fiance

Her Marine Daddy

Her Dueling Daddies

Beauty & The Lumberjacks

Innocence: a dark mafia romance trilogy with Stasia Black

Beauty's Beast: a dark romance with Stasia Black

ABOUT LEE SAVINO

Lee Savino is a USA today bestselling author of smexy romance. Smexy, as in "smart and sexy." Find her in the Goddess Group on facebook and download a free book at www.leesavino.com!

If you want more menage, check out the Draekon series. If you want more sexy (spanko) werewolves, check out my Alpha series. Lee has more books but those two series should hold you for awhile. ;)

Find her at:
www.leesavino.com

Lightning Source UK Ltd.
Milton Keynes UK
UKHW012044290821
389674UK00002B/460